FINN

SECRETS AND LIES BOOK 3

B J ALPHA

BJ Alpha
x

Published by BJ Alpha

Edited by Sam O'Neill

Cover Design by Katie Evans

❀ Created with Vellum

FINN

BJALPHA

PLAYLIST

Lost Without You - Freya Riding
Wait for You - Tom Walker (Acoustic)
Always Been You - Jessie Murph
I Won't Give Up - Jason Mraz
Can You Hold Me - Britt Nicole
Everything I didn't Say - Ella Henderson
Fight Song - Rachel Platten
By Your Side - Calvin Harris
Here With Me - Marshmello

My Girl - Elvie Shane
Dedicated to all the Charlie's in the world.
Blood doesn't make a father, love does.

AUTHORS NOTE

WARNING:

This book contains triggers. It contains sensitive and explicit storylines such as graphic sexual scenes and abuse, scenes of human trafficking and dubious consent.

The book contains strong, offensive language and therefore is recommended for ages eighteen and over.

What you've endured does not define who you are.
You're here.
You are a survivor.

BJ Alpha

PROLOGUE

Finn

I'm balls deep in the long-haired fake blonde. Roughly tugging her hair back, it's wrapped around my hand like a god damn chain; I thrust harder into her. Her moans make my teeth clench with annoyance. Why can't she just shut the fuck up? Why can't they ever just let me get inside my head and let me enjoy what the fuck I'm imagining?

I'm going at her harder from behind. Not because I'm losing control, not because I'm enjoying myself, it's because I can't wait for it to finish so she can just fuck off.

My phone buzzes from the nightstand, great another fucking distraction. I squeeze my eyes shut to rein in my temper. Luckily, I don't recognize the ringtone, which means it's no one important. I don't bother to answer it, letting it go to voicemail. Eventually, it stops ringing. Good, now I can get back to fucking business and get this over with.

"Ah, yes," she moans again, louder than before. I grind my teeth.

"I told you to shut the fuck up and keep your fucking head down!" I grit out, my jaw popping with the tension

1

behind my bite, annoyance taking over what's meant to be the high.

She does as she's told with another moan. I'm not sure whether that's a satisfied moan, or a disgruntled moan, but what the fuck ever, just let me finish already.

I close my eyes and concentrate harder, grinding my teeth to pinpoint the memories. Angel on all fours with me pounding into her tight little ass, her tight little pussy sucking me in. Fuck yes... All of a sudden, I can't control myself, the rush liberating just from her memory alone. "I'm coming." I grit out the words as if it pains me to admit she's managed to get me off. My cock is still pulsating, but I ignore it and before I let her finish, I pull out of her abruptly, rip the condom off and storm to the bathroom, my hands now covered in cum. Disappointment and guilt curdle inside me. The only person I want to fuck left me. I hate her, but I love her more—more than she loved me. A wave of sickness clogs in my throat, spurring me into action.

I wash my face with the ice-cold water to bring me back to reality; avoiding the mirror above the sink, I throw the condom in the bin, pull on some boxers, and swing open the door.

The blond is sitting up, tucked under the duvet, with the comforter pulled above her breasts. Trying to look all sweet and innocent. Does she think she's staying the night? Err, yeah, wrong there darlin'.

I pick her skimpy dress up off the floor and throw it at her. "Get dressed and get the fuck out!" I spit at her, tilting my head toward the door.

Her face turns murderous. "What? Are you kidding me right now? We just fucked!" She screeches, rage burning behind her eyes.

"Yeah, I'm aware of what we did. You've served your purpose; now fuck off!" Again, I nod at the door.

She huffs, grumbling words under her breath. She storms

around the room and starts getting dressed. I stand and watch her with my arms folded across my chest. I need to make sure she's got the fucking message, and she leaves.

Before now, I've had chicks climb back into my bed when I turn my back. One bitch took longer to get rid of than it took me to come. How the fuck is that fair?

I stick a toothpick in my mouth. It's kind of my signature thing. I stopped smoking once I got out of the forces, and for some reason, took this habit up. I don't realize I'm doing it most of the time, but having something in my mouth, moving it around, biting down on it, it soothes me in a way that smoking did.

Angel hated me smoking. That's another reason why I gave it up. For her. I did everything for her. I scrub a hand through my hair aggravated my mind went to her once again.

The door slams and the blonde is gone. My shoulders relax slightly with her disappearance. I pour myself another drink from the bar and sit beside the bed. Tension is still tightly coiled around my body that the orgasm barely helped relieve. Why the fuck can't I feel the euphoria I did with Angel? I scrub a hand down my face in annoyance. Picking up my phone, I head out onto the balcony.

Glancing down at my phone, I've got three missed calls from a number I don't recognize. It's a Michigan number. I frown as I call the voicemail service and listen. *'Hello, this is a message for a Mr. Finnley O'Connell. My name is Marcy Fullen, calling from the University of Michigan Hospital; we have a patient by the name of Chelsea Danes with us who, unfortunately, has been involved in a road traffic collision. As her next of kin, could you please contact us as soon as possible for further details? Thank you.'*

What the fuck? Michigan? Hospital? Who the fuck is Chelsea Danes? I shake my head and try to think who the fuck just called me and how they got my name right, but all the other facts are wrong. This is either a prank or some

3

serious fucked up coincidence. I shake my head and down my drink. Time to get the fuck out of here.

Thankfully, I don't have many things to pack up. I've only been in this hotel for the past two nights. I can't wait to get in my own bed away from all this superficial bullshit.

I hope, to fucking Christ, Oscar is waiting for me when I land at the helipad. What am I thinking? Of course, he is; he cannot stand anyone being late, which is probably why he and Con clash so much; he's always been shit at punctuality, especially since having Will and Keen back in his life and now he has the fucking rat dog too. He has a perfect excuse every time he's late, family. An emptiness overcomes me, the feeling of what should have been. That should have been me and Angel, kids and a dog. My shoulders slump in defeat.

———

The airport doors open, and I breathe in the fresh air. Granted, it's not the best, but compared to being holed up in New York for two nights, well, New Jersey is a fucking dream.

Oscar is in his blacked-out SUV, his glasses on and eyes narrowed at me. Jeez, he's always so fucking intense; no wonder I'm always on a knife's edge and struggle to relax.

I open the passenger door and throw my bag in the back. "Why not put it in the trunk?" He glares at me.

I breathe out. I mean, seriously, I've been away for two fucking nights, forced to dress up as a pompous prick at charity events for the good of this family, and the first thing he says to me is a fucking insult.

I decide not to bite. I ignore the prick and turn the music up. Oscar just as quickly turns it down. "So, how'd it go?"

I sigh and throw my head back against the passenger seat, rolling my head toward him. "Seriously Oscar, it was a fucking charity event. How the fuck do you think it went?

Bor-fuckin-ing. If Cal could just get his shit together and just leave his goddamn family for five minutes, maybe, we could all go back to our roles in the family and I wouldn't have to fly here, there and every fucking where and play the fucking city saint!" My hands fling out as I speak to him.

Oscar's lips quirk, which is equivalent to a laugh. "That good?"

I nod in response, just as my cell starts buzzing. I fidget to pull it out from within my jacket pocket, nearly dropping my toothpick in the process. I sigh, not recognizing the number. "Yeah," I answer nonchalantly.

"Hello there, am I speaking to a Mr. Finnley O'Connell?" A chirpy voice replies.

"Yeah, you are." I must look confused, because Oscar throws me a suspicious glance.

"Oh, thank goodness, you're speaking to Susan at the University of Michigan Hospital; please don't worry straight away, but we do have a Chelsea Danes in our care here and as her next of kin, you're our first port of contact...."

Rubbing at my forehead, I blow out an audible breath. I don't let her finish. "Look lady, I haven't got a clue who this Chelsea chick is. I've never heard of her before, I mean, she might be some bird I've screwed, but I really don't want to be her next of kin, so if you can just cross me off the fucking list and pass this shit on to someone that gives a fuck that would be great." I end the call.

Oscar turns to me with a raised eyebrow.

I shrug, "Haven't got a fucking clue bro, so don't ask. That's the second time they've called, claiming they have someone in their care and I'm their next of kin. Some fucking scam or something wanting me to pay the bill, mark my words!" I point at Oscar with emphasis, confident in my assessment of the phone call. Yeah, definitely a scam.

Oscar nods in agreement. He clears his throat, appearing a bit awkward. "Do you want to head to the bar and grab something to eat? Or go straight home?" He asks with uncertainty, his eyes darting between mine and the road ahead.

"Fuck, I need a drink, bro. You good with that?"

Oscar's lips turn up in what resembles a smile and nods.

Out of all my brothers, Oscar is the one I'm the least close to, but to be fair, he's very guarded and damn right odd. As we've got older, we came to realize that Oscar has issues, and when I mean issues, I mean fucking issues. He's clearly got something wrong with him. Nowadays, his issues would be addressed and given names and pills, but growing up when we did, in the home we grew up in, the poor kid retreated and became known as the weirdo and the odd one out.

Since discovering we have a nephew 'Reece,' Cal's son. Who also just so happens to have 'issues,' we've been a lot more accommodating and determined to support Oscar. So, when he asks if we want to go somewhere for a drink or something to eat? Really, he means he wants to go. Will we join him?

————

Settled in the booth with a beer in one hand and my bowl of fries in the other, we both relax watching the New York Giants hammer the LA Rams. My phone starts dancing across the table. Glancing at the screen, unknown number, I sneer at the fucking phone.

"Yes!" I snap.

"Hello Sir, am I speaking to a Mr. Finnley O'Connell?"

I seethe, catching Oscar's razor-sharp focus on me. He mouths at me to put it on speaker. I just start to wonder what he's doing when he pulls his tablet out from under the table and gives me a knowing smirk. Yes! Oscar's going to track the fucker and they'll be fucking sorry. I smile back and play along with this little game.

"Yes, this is Mr. O'Connell," I reply in a patronizing tone.

"Oh excellent, we've really struggled to get a hold of you, Mr. O'Connell; you sure are a tough cookie to track…" *yeah, she's no fucking idea.*

"My name is Marcy, and I'm calling from the University of Michigan Hospital. I'm very sorry to inform you we have a Chelsea Danes in our care at the minute," she waits for me to say something.

"Oh, Chelsea. Wow, that's tragic. Is she dying?" I ask, raising a smirk to my own face as Oscar stares at me with a humorous glint in his eye. He rolls his hand forward in a motion to get me to continue the conversation, giving him a chance to work.

"Oh no, Mr. O'Connell, thankfully Chelsea is out of danger now, but she has received some serious injuries and is now recovering well in our care."

"Could you tell me the details so I can visit poor Chelsea?" I try to make my voice sound as sympathetic as possible.

"Of course, Mr. O'Connell, she will be in our care for the next few days and she's staying in room fourteen, level seven, in the St Mary's Wing. Shall I let her know you've been contacted when she wakes?" Wow, this lady is good. She sure means business getting my money.

I peer up at Oscar. He tilts his head down sharply to say he's tracked the call and I can now finish this dumb conversation.

"No, no need to tell her, Marcy. I'll be there soon, thank you." I can be sickly sweet when I try.

Putting my phone down, I meet Oscar's eyes. He's tapping away and then his eyebrows narrow in a telltale sign of confusion.

I sigh, "Go on then, give it to me. What have you got?"

He moves around to my side of the booth and I push my plate away to make room for his tablet. "So, I've located the call; it's definitely from the hospital. I've registered the caller,

Marcy Fullen again she's legit and I've tracked down the so-called patient, Chelsea Danes, again; all true, she's a patient there." I'm starting to wonder what the fuck's going on, but knowing Oscar, he'll have it all resolved in a second. Slowly, I take a swig of my beer, going over in my mind what Oscar is saying.

"I'm just tracking this Chelsea Danes. Her details and an ID photo should be up any minute, then you'll know which woman you've scorned and who is trying to get you to pay the bill," He says with a snarl. Ever the advocate for how to treat a woman, I roll my eyes at him.

Oscar is not a fan of mine and what used to be Con's playboy ways. I'm not sure what he expects from me, but I don't do relationships. He gives me the impression he finds it disgusting that I fuck around, but hey, I'm not the one that pays for sex.

I laugh at Oscar's comment. Clearly, we've both drawn the same conclusion. I've upset some bird, and she's using this as payback.

Oscar stands and points to the tablet. "I'm just going to use the restroom; keep an eye on the tablet. The name is being tracked, and any images in the system will bounce back anytime now." I nod in acknowledgment.

Taking another swig of my beer and another one of my cold fries, my eyes scan over the room before I glance back down toward the screen. The screen flickers as if it is updating and up pops an image. Here goes... my eyes narrow as the image uploads.

My body stills as I stare at the girl in the image. I can't breathe, my stomach plummets, my body feels heavy, and my mind is blank. I go to pick the tablet up, but I can't. My mind and fingers don't seem to match. With shaky hands, I zoom in on the ID. She's there. On the screen. The screen in front of me.

For some stupid reason, I look around the bar like someone's playing a prank on me.

Staring back at the photo ID, she's actually fucking there. My eyes feel heavy, watery. What the fuck is wrong with me? I can't process what's happening.

"Finn!" Oscar barks, looming from above me. "What's wrong? I've said your name a thousand times." He snaps.

I gaze at him, confused. Where the fuck am I? What the fuck is happening? Why is she on the fucking screen? Why is she called fucking Chelsea?

Oscar's eyes assess me and he must see something on my face that resembles panic. He quickly sits back down and goes to snatch the tablet, but I grab his hand forcefully to stop him.

I don't want him to knock her face from the screen; I don't want him to touch her. Shit, what the fuck's happening? I hate losing control like this.

"It's okay, let me see," Oscar says, gently coaxing the screen from me as if I'm a child. He's got worry in his eyes and I know it's because he's never seen me react to any situation like this before. Honestly? I mean, I never have.

Oscar gazes down at the screen and then back at me with a face of pure shock and confusion. "Angel?"

I nod. "What the fuck's happening Oscar? That's her, right? She's on the fucking screen! Why does it say her name's Chelsea?" My voice comes out shaky and unsure. Nothing like me; I'm normally strong, resilient and a fucking hard ass. Not a meek, sappy fucking twat.

Oscar clears his throat, glancing down and then back at me. "You're right, it's her Finn. It's Angel. She's clearly using another name." He rolls his teeth between his lip as if in thought.

I sit and think for a second. I assumed the name was wrong, but that makes more sense now. But why? Why the fuck would she use another name? And why the fuck is her hair a different color? Her fucking long blonde, almost white hair, was beautiful. She looked like a goddamn goddess, my fucking beautiful, innocent Angel. Anger builds inside me. How dare she change her hair?

As if now only registering the importance of the phone call, panic roils through me. "Shit. She's hurt. Shit, Oscar, do I call the hospital back? I need to see her!" My heart is pounding against my chest. The toothpick dropped from my mouth. I keep brushing my hand through my already messy hair. Shit, she's hurt.

Oscar's dark, no-nonsense voice breaks my thought of panic. His eyes hold mine. "No. Finn, if you want to see her, just go to her. You don't know why she's changed her name. So just go to her." I nod in agreement. He grabs my arm, looking deep into my eyes pointedly, "Tell no one."

My spine straightens at his pointed words. I bring my eyes up to meet Oscar's and narrow them in confusion. A wave of uncertainty overcomes me, and a pool of dread whirls deep inside. Why, if she's put me as her next of kin, would he think I shouldn't let her know I'm coming?

Oscar must read my mind, "Finn, this ID is fake. She's no other ID in her original name or this fake one. No bank account, no social security number, nothing. It's like she doesn't exist." He winces at his own words.

My body jolts in shock at registering what Oscar is telling me.

What the fuck? I thought she was happily married on the West fucking coast! What the fuck is happening?

"You think she's in trouble? You're saying she's in trouble, right?" My eyes frantically search his face for answers.

Oscar nods. "Yeah, man, I'm sorry, but I think she's in trouble. Nothing else makes any sense. I can't find any address, like ever. She's never existed until this point. Until we know what's happening, you need to keep a low profile too. Use burners, cash only. Let's just see what the fuck all this is about and then we can take the heat off, okay?" I drop my head sharply in agreement.

Oscar's right; until I speak to Angel and know what kind of trouble she's in, we have to assume that those people now know I've been contacted and therefore might be seen as an extension of her troubles. Jesus.

"Okay. So Da's going to be pissed, but the chopper is being refueled as we speak, and I've booked you a car and hotel. You are going to see her, right? Get answers?" Oscar says with hope in his eyes.

I raise an eyebrow. Did he seriously just ask me that? This is my chance. This is it. She's coming home where she belongs. She's coming home to me, whether she likes it or not —my lip curls at the side with the thought of Angel back where she belongs.

Oscar smirks back at me. That fucking cocky lob-sided smirk mirrored my own.

CHAPTER 1

F **inn**

    I hate fucking hospitals; I know everyone does, right? My body is rigid as I make my way down the endless corridors.

I'm in St Mary's Hospital, on level seven, and it's fucking busy, real fucking busy.

I'm getting knocked from side to side with all the hustle and bustle. Doctors, nurses, patients, family members, police officers and crying kids. Jesus, it's hell.

This shit hole makes me fucking grateful for the private facilities that my family can afford.

I glance at each door number as I make my way along the corridor. Dodging a bed trolley here and there.

I finally get to room fourteen and hope to hell she hasn't been moved. The blind is down on the door, so I can't see inside. I bounce nervously on my heels. I have my hand on the handle, a little unsure whether or not to knock. Will she be pleased to see me?

My heart is pounding in my chest, anxiety rippling through me. Standing there, I tell myself, I can do this. I can fucking do it.

Pushing the door handle down, I step into the room; it's dark. My eyes try to adjust to the lack of lighting.

The bed is directly in front of me. A quick glance around and I see a chair to the right; a door behind it must lead to the shower room. The blinds above the bed are closed, making the room even darker, which means I can't see her properly. I'm not even convinced it's her. I scrub a hand through my hair and lick my lips nervously, the sound of my thumping heart echoing in my ears.

The girl is completely still in the bed, clearly sleeping. I move closer for a better look. Slowly making my way over to the chair beside the bed, "Angel." I ask as I quietly approach.

She doesn't respond.

When I get to her, I stand over her sleeping form; I scan her body over and my knees almost buckle. It's her! It's fucking her. My fucking Angel! I can't control my hands as they shake uncontrollably; my chest rises and falls rapidly. My throat is suddenly so fucking dry it hurts. It's her.

I scrutinize her face. Only it's not her…

Angel doesn't look like Angel anymore. What the ever-loving fuck? My mouth drops open in disgust. My blood starts to boil, and my anxiety is soon dispersed to make way for anger. Sheer fucking anger.

Her hair is still long but dark red. Red? Like bottle red, cherry fucking red.

She has some fresh cuts to her face, probably from the collision. She has tattoos all the way down her left arm, stopping at her wrist. Fucking tattoos? I grind my teeth. The Angel I knew didn't like a blemish on her skin. It was fucking flawless, let alone having a fucking tattoo. My jaw aches, my muscles coiled tight. What the hell was she thinking? Her frame is still small, but her hospital gown is tight across her chest, which means her tits are big. Did she have a tit job? She best not have had a fucking tit job. Her tits were perfect, absolutely fucking perfect.

I scan her body up and down again, taking her all in. My fists clench beside me. How fucking dare she change herself like this? Angel was fucking perfect. Anger flows through my veins at her decision to alter herself.

She's got a piercing in her nose, a fucking piercing. Multiple in her right ear. My mouth gapes open. I didn't let her have her ears pierced. They were fucking perfect as they were. Why the fuck has she changed everything? What the hell is happening? This is some twilight zone shit going off here. I can feel my heart race. I don't know if it's anxiety or anger now. My mind is so fucked up in shock. I glance at the door. Do they realize how much she's changed?

"Angel?" I ask again, a bite to my tone. Still no response.

I glance at her IV drip and decide she must be out for the fucking count on pain killers. I gaze around the room, unsure whether to track a doctor down and demand answers, but then I glance at her again and I don't want to fucking leave her.

I decide to sit on the chair beside her and wait for her to wake. Then she can fucking explain herself to me. All these fucking changes she's made. Unnecessary fucking changes. I shake my head in disgust.

Sitting beside her, I gently take her hand in mine. It's warm and dainty, just how I remember her. I squeeze my eyes shut at the memory, absolutely dumbfounded that I've found my girl. I finally fucking have her and I'm never letting her go again. Ever.

Opening my eyes, I struggle to look away from her beautiful sleeping face. She's still there, still my Angel. I stroke my thumb over her hand. It's something I've always done with her, and now, more than eight years later, it feels like yesterday when I last did it.

I'll never let her go again, that's for sure. She's mine now. Mine.

When she wakes, she's got some fucking explaining to do.

———

My head drops, startling me. I must have fallen asleep; it's been a long-ass fucking day.

A ripple of panic runs through me. Did I dream about it? My eyes dart up toward my hand; it's still entwined with hers. Large roses flow up her arm, covering her skin, causing me to grimace. I don't dislike them. But I was expecting to see her pale, flawless skin beside mine. But she's here, thank god she's here, I can live with the fucking tattoos if it means having her here; the thought consoles me.

I shuffle. Hospital chairs are fucking uncomfortable, restlessness now settling in on me. I need answers, and I need her to wake up. What if she can't remember me? Panic begins to build inside me. Jesus, Finn, calm the fuck down. I'll just fuck the memories back into her.

I look around the room, trying to figure out what's happening. Did nobody come in to check on her? Does she need more medication? I need to get her moved to somewhere with decent facilities, where she can get the attention she needs.

Stretching my arms above my head, I push back the chair and stand. My eyes lock on her bed. I really need to piss, but I don't want to leave her. Fuck, my hands rub my forehead in unease.

I reluctantly glance at the door behind me. Jesus Finn, get a grip, it's a quick piss and then you're back.

Bending down, I kiss her forehead. "Back in a minute, Angel." I breathe in her scent. Fucking strawberries, always fucking strawberries. I smile to myself. She's back. She's actually fucking back.

After taking the longest piss known to man, I wash my face with freezing water to freshen myself up, dry my hands on the paper towel and then go back out.

My shoulders sag in relief to see she hasn't fucking moved an inch.

I sit back in the chair. Just as I stretch my legs out in front of me, I hear a click and then automatically feel the cold end of a Glock touching the side of my head. Immediately, I tense, my senses on high alert.

"Who the fuck are you? What are you doing in here?" A man's voice snaps. I can see from the shadow beside me that the figure is tall. Not as tall as me, though, I'm six foot two. He appears lean too, so if I can get him to lower his gun, I can take him.

"Hospital called me. I'm her next of kin." I tilt my head slightly toward Angel's bed.

The voice scoffs, "Bull shit. Do you really expect me to believe that? I'm her brother."

"Believe what the fuck you want, it's the truth, and for the record, she hasn't got a brother." I snark back, knowingly.

Silence.

"I know Chelsea; the hospital wouldn't have called you. I'm not stupid," he splutters.

Now it's my turn to scoff. Clearly, he's stupid. "Well, clearly, you are stupid. You're holding a gun to my head. Her name's not Chelsea, and the hospital called me relentlessly." I say a little louder, bolder, completely undeterred by the gun pointed at my head.

He shuffles from side to side, showing he's unsure about the situation.

"How do you know Chelsea? And what's your name, prick?" He says, standing taller but feigning confidence.

I bite the inside of my mouth. Yeah, ideally, I need a tooth-pick to chew on but can't move a fucking muscle incase this guy thinks I'm pulling a weapon on him. This douche is really pissing me off!

"My names Finn O'Connell. The hospital called me to say

17

I'm her next of kin; not sure how or why, but I am. And that right there is Angel, not fucking Chelsea." I snap back. Fucking Chelsea? I ain't calling her that shit, no matter what she's told this douche.

He releases a sharp intake of breath, stepping back slightly. He's panicking, "Shit, shit, shit!" He chants. "You said the hospital called you? When? H... h... have you told anyone else she's here? Shit, this is a fucking disaster." The dude is hyperventilating. Luckily, he's dropped the gun from the side of my head. I turn and give him my full attention now. He's in tight jeans and has a hoodie on. He's lean like I predicted, not muscled. Maybe 5 foot 11. Brown hair cut neatly at the sides and slight length on top; he has a slim face with no scars.

"You gonna tell me why the fuck you pointed a gun at my head? And why the fuck you're freaking out?" I snide out.

"Oh. My. God, I'm so sorry!" He screeches out in a low feminine voice. He becomes all animated with his hands, making me nervous as hell. The dudes still got a gun in his hand, for Christ's sake. "So, it's nice to finally meet you Finn, and aren't you the little fitty? My name is Tyler, but my friends call me Ty. I'm Chelsea's BFF." He rambles off. I've never heard anyone talk so fast. He's all excitable and shit too.

I stare at him wide-eyed, confused the fuck out. He's gone from a psychotic killer to prancing around talking animated. What the fuck is this bullshit? What the hell is happening? My tone darkens in rage at having a gun pulled on me and having no fucking answers about what the hell is happening. "Okay, so back the fuck up. What the hell's a BFF?"

This Tyler guy throws his head back and giggles. Fucking giggles! "Oh my god, you're so cute." He throws his head back, giggling at me? "Best Friend Forever, obvs."

I shake my head. Is he for real? I stare at him. He winks at me. Yeah, he's for real. Jesus. I backtrack on his words. Hold the fuck up. Cute? I'm fucking cute? I'm anything but fucking cute.

Scrubbing a hand down my face, I exhale in frustration. Softening my tone because Tyler seems like an okay guy; when he isn't pointing a gun at my head, plus, I might get some answers, finally. "Tyler, dude," I breathe out loudly. "I'll be honest with you. Seriously, I haven't got a fucking clue what's happening here. The hospital called me and told me I'm Angel's next of kin. I come here after last seeing her over eight fucking years ago." My voice becomes a little more pissed as I point toward Angel, "and this girl in the bed looks nothing like the Angel I know. I take a piss; you point a gun to my head and now you're all excited and it's freaking me the fuck out!" I exhale sharply, hoping he can hear how desperate I am for answers.

Tyler is quiet, appearing deep in thought. Before he visually snaps himself out of it. Then he goes over to the door and moves the blinds slightly. He turns quickly back toward me with a panicked expression. "The police are out there," he whispers, his eyes widening in panic.

I nod in understanding. "And?"

He meets my eyes with an expression of confusion before he shakes his head slightly, as if coming to his senses. Then he begins pacing. "Okay, so she's just got a concussion and bruising, right? So, you stay with Angel." He turns back to me, eyes meeting mine with all seriousness, "Don't let anyone question her Finn, let nobody in this room." He points to the floor while looking at me pointedly. "As soon as you can, you need to get her out of here. Tell her that Tyler has sorted Charlie and to meet back at Chad's, okay?"

My back straightens. "Wait, what the fuck is happening? Who and what the fuck are Chad and Charlie, and where the fuck are you going?" I ask, my voice desperate for someone to tell me what's happening.

He ignores my questions. "I brought her a bag with a few

clothes. Here, I'll leave her my hoodie." He takes his hoodie off and leaves it on the bed as he hurriedly walks around the room.

I dart toward him. There's no fucking way he's leaving here after dropping those little bombshells without explanation. Gripping his arm, I all but beg, "Tyler, man, what the fuck's happening?" Desperation seeping through my voice.

He stares at me with pity in his eyes. As if unsure of what to do or say, he's fidgeting from side to side on his feet, occasionally glancing back at the door.

He lowers his voice. "Finn, you have to promise not to tell anyone she's here. You need to swear it, Finn. It's a matter of life and death." His eyes drill into me with severity.

I swallow thickly, a wave of sickness washing over me. My stomach is knotting at the thought that Angel could be in some serious shit, and nobody is giving me any facts. I swallow thickly, "of course, I'll protect her with my life." I tell him with all sincerity.

Tyler's eyes trace over my face, then he nods, pleased with my response. He rushes over to the bed, kisses Angel on her forehead, and almost stumbles past me. "Look after her," his voice is gentle, laced with worry. Then he leaves and closes the door with a soft click. My answers are gone with him. I exhale, scrubbing my hand down my face. I put a toothpick in my mouth to calm myself.

I stare at the bed, then back toward the door. What the fuck just happened?

———

It feels like hours, but in reality, it's probably only been an hour. No fucker has been to check on Angel, which I guess, given the circumstance that Tyler alluded to, it's probably a good thing.

Angel moves her head slowly from side to side, mumbling. I quickly sit forward, my heart racing a mile a minute. I gently move the hair away from her eyes, "Angel, can you hear me? Angel?" I speak in a low, soft voice.

"Finn?" Her dainty voice breathes, sending a flutter in my chest like a teenager.

I smile, a big fucking smile, "yeah, it's me, Angel."

Her eyes shoot open, she stares directly at me. Then she closes them again. Takes a deep breath as if preparing herself. Her chest rises rapidly and then she opens her eyes once again. "Finn?"

"Yeah, Angel, it's me," I smirk at her response.

Her eyes dart manically around the room, "You're here? In front of me? In this room?"

I chuckle at her response. So fucking cute. "Yeah, I'm here darlin'. You're in the hospital."

"The hospital? What the fuck?" She sits up but quickly drops back with a hand to her forehead. "My head hurts. What am I doing?" She scrunches her nose up.

I laugh because she looks so damn adorable when she's confused. "You're in the hospital, darlin'. Apparently, you had a road traffic collision. Do you remember any of that?"

Angel is silent. Her eyebrows furrow as though she's deep in thought. "I think I crashed the car."

I laugh. I can't even imagine her driving a car. She was always too timid to do anything and she sure as hell wouldn't drive my car when I offered to teach her.

"Perhaps you need lessons?" I joke.

She narrows her eyes at me, sitting up. "Very fucking funny. Now, what the hell are you doing here?" She snaps at me. My spine straightens in temper. Wow, there's me, hoping she'd be pleased to see me.

My tone darkens. "I'm your next of kin, Angel. But you know that already, don't you? Given the fact you'd have put my name on your forms, am I right?" I wriggle my eyebrows at her, proud that she obviously forgot that little bit of information.

"I put your name on my forms so you'd know when I died, asshole. Not when I had a minor bump in the road." She snarks back.

My eyes bug out at her response, shaking my head, surprised at her attitude. I swipe my finger over my lip, enjoying toying with her again. "Mmm, whatever you say, someone didn't get that memo. Anyway, why the fuck are you putting a different name on your medical forms?" I ask her, determined to get some answers.

She goes tense. Her back is rigid and her body stills. A look of horror crosses over her face, suddenly realizing I know more than I'm supposed to.

She begins to panic, the heart rate monitor going haywire. "I need to get out of here. Shit, I'm such a fucking idiot." She pulls the IV drip from her arm without flinching. Then proceeds to sit up to get off the bed, swaying slightly in the process.

I hold up my hand to stop her. "Wow, hold the fuck up! You're not going anywhere, not yet anyway. You've got some fucking explaining to do." I clench my teeth in annoyance. If she thinks she can run out of here without an explanation, she can think A. Fucking. Gain.

"Like fuck I have. I need to get out of here." Her eyes dart frantically around the room.

Using my body, I block her from getting off the bed. I change my voice to placate her, "Look, I spoke to Tyler, and he left a message with me, but I'm going to need you to tell me what the fuck's going on for you to get that message, okay?" I cross my arms, grinning, pleased I have a little blackmail to get what I want.

Angel stares at me in shock, her mouth dropping open, "You spoke to Tyler?"

"Yeah, I did." I grin smugly.

"Wh… what did he say?" She asks nervously, chewing her finger, ducking her eyes away from me.

"First, tell me what the fuck is happening." I demand, deepening my tone.

She glances around the room, as if she's looking for answers. She takes a deep breath. "I might have stolen a car and accidentally crashed it." Angel winces at her words.

I nod sharply, both in acknowledgment and shock. She stole a fucking car? Where the fuck is my Angel? Like my literal Angel, not this Angel. I'm so fucking angry right now. My jaw ticks and my temple pulsates. This is not what I wanted for her, not at all.

Her beautiful green eyes peer up at me in disappointment.

I stroke her cheek, the action causing tingles to spread through my body. I have my beautiful girl back; she leans into my touch. "Hey, it's okay. Don't worry. Whatever this is, we can sort it." I wave my hand around the room.

She shakes her head and quickly turns away. She swallows harshly. "No, we can't sort it. Nothing can be sorted." Her voice laced with sadness and defeat.

My spine straightens, determined to show her. Prove to her that I can resolve her problems, "Angel…"

Her firm voice cuts me off. "No Finn, don't call me that…" she shakes her head and tugs on her hair. "Please don't call me that. I'm not Angel anymore. Don't you see? I'm not that person anymore. You can't just come here and expect me to be. Things have changed."

I take a step back, jolting at her words. Of course, I can fucking see. But she's still my girl, mine. "Yeah, I can see a whole lot fucking changed." I snipe, gesturing at her.

She takes a deep breath and pushes off the bed again, refusing to acknowledge my words. "Now, what the fuck did Tyler say?"

My eyebrows shoot up. Wow, she fucking swears too?

I clear my throat as she stomps around the room, gathering the clothes together. I begrudgingly relay Tyler's words. "He said he's got Charlie and he'll see you at Chad's." Her eyes snap to mine at the mention of Charlie, and she stills. What the fuck's all that about? Who the fuck is Charlie? If she has a boyfriend, he's a dead man.

"Is that it?" she glares at me, the attitude back in full force.

"Yeah, and just instructions for me to look after you and not mention you to anyone."

She stops what she's doing again and turns to face me, giving me her full attention. She swallows heavily. "And did you?"

I drag a hand through my hair, getting frustrated with the multitude of questions but no answers. "Did I what?"

"Mention me to anyone?" Her eyes don't leave my face, searching for answers.

I laugh sarcastically, "No darlin', of course not."

"So, nobody knows you're here, right?" She asks again with an analyzing stare.

I scratch my head. "I mean, Oscar knows, but he wouldn't tell anyone."

She drops the bag of clothes and stumbles a little in shock. "Oscar knows?" She snaps.

I shrug. "Yeah, but you don't have to worry about him, darlin'."

She shakes her head. "I'm not worried about Oscar. I'm worried about who else might know." Well, that was fucking cryptic.

I lick my lips as I scan her hot body, completely unperturbed by Angel's panic mode. "Angel, seriously, you're worrying for no fucking reason. Nobody knows, I swear."

She tilts her head in acknowledgment, but it's clear she isn't convinced. Her eyes dart away again. She's keeping something from me, that's for sure.

The next thing I know, she pulls the hospital gown over

her head, making me step back in shock. The old Angel would have gone into the restroom. This Angel doesn't give a shit.

Oh, my fucking god, she's got curves in all the right places. How the fuck did she get curves? My throat clogs and suddenly, I can't swallow. My cock twitches as my eyes rake over her delicious body. Her full, heavy tits are fucking huge compared to eight years ago; on closer inspection, yeah, they're fucking huge! My cock swells and I can't take my eyes away from the beauties.

Jesus, her nipple is pierced. What the fuck? She's walking around, mumbling to herself, pulling the clothes out of the bag. Me? I'm standing here dumbstruck, like a fucking teenager with the biggest fucking hard-on. I rub at my cock, annoyingly to take away the need. I can't think past the fact she's fucking amazing. So beautiful, stunning. Mine.

"You're staring," she grumbles while slowly dressing in the clothes, not even acknowledging me with her eyes.

"Your tits grew." I point out while staring directly at them.

"No shit! They're huge, right?" She grins proudly, biting her bottom lip. Fuck, I could suck on that lip. My heart hammers at the thought.

"They real?" I quirk a brow. I'm not sure I actually want an answer to that.

"I stole a car, Finn. Do you actually think I'd have the money for a tit job?" She laughs playfully.

I stand staring at her in utter shock. I shrug and then gulp, "they were fine before. But I mean, they're okay now." Yeah, okay, I'm playing it down. They're incredible.

"They're okay?" She huffs, "wow, not the reaction I normally get from guys but whatever." She shrugs nonchalantly.

Guys? What fucking guys? Fuck, why the fuck did she have to say that? I avert my gaze because, yeah, I'm pissed right now. My jaw works from side to side. I need a fucking cigarette. That's what I need. I'd also like nothing more than to pin her down and spurt my cum all over her fucking tits so every fucker can smell me on her. Then they'd know she's mine, that's for sure. My cock leaks against my denim-clad leg, imagining her covered in my cum.

I snap out of my thoughts, watching her slide on some battered converse, "look, if you could do me a stellar favor and help me get out of here without being detected by the police, I'd be sincerely grateful." She tilts her head toward the door while writing something on a piece of paper she ripped off her medical file while I was daydreaming about her covered in my cum.

"Are you going to tell me what the hell's going on? Why you changed your name and shit? Tell me everything?"

She shrugs, "Sure." Her eyes were still concentrating on the paper.

Once she's dressed, she tugs on the hoodie.

Slowly, Angel walks over to me. It's the first time she's properly made eye contact with me, her green eyes transfixed to mine, holding me in place. Her throat moves harshly with emotion, her hand reaches for my face, and I let her brush her fingers down my cheek and tenderly over my jawline. I close my eyes briefly, my heart racing. She places her palm over my heart knowingly and I cover it with mine. It's our way of saying, "I love you," because we were both too young and dumb to ever utter the words. I wince at the pain in my chest, regretting never saying them.

We haven't seen each other for so long and we're having that moment. A moment where I can see the pain in her eyes and she can see the pain in mine. She can see into my soul, my very core, the real me. Right there and then, I know I won't let her leave me again, never again. My body fills with determination to get her onboard with the idea. I'm going nowhere and neither is she.

Angel's eyes fill with tears, and she quickly averts her

gaze. I grab her hand before she can move away from me. "Talk to me." My throat works as I practically beg. Because I sure as shit know there's a lot going on, and I want to make it right for her.

She nods and turns her back on me. "Later," she mumbles.

CHAPTER 2

Angel

"Later." I agree, knowing full well I'm lying. I brush the feeling of guilt aside, the desperation to keep him.

I shake my head at my own stupidity. Of course, I can't keep him. They'll find me if I keep him, and then they'll find out what happened. No. I have to let him go again. My hands shake with emotion, the tingling of his heart beating against my palm still there. I lick my lips and move forward with the plan.

Composing myself, I open the door with a renewed sense of vigor, carefully poking my head out to peer up and down the corridor, my blood pulsing heavily around my veins.

"Put your hood up and tuck your hair inside the hoodie. The whole red thing you've got going on is hot, but not exactly inconspicuous." I can sense Finn smiling at his own words. I grimace at the pain in my chest, the pain of my heart breaking all over again. And he's absolutely no idea it's about to happen.

I duck my head in shame and do as instructed. Finn takes

my hand in his, his large palm encompassing my small hand. Loving the feel of him, I struggle to keep my emotions in check as he pushes us through the door. Finn's voice drops to a whisper. "Keep your eyes down. If I see the police, I'll squeeze your hand and we will change direction, okay?" I nod in agreement.

Walking down the corridor, it's actually quiet, doctors are sparse now and odd staff mill around. A sense of unease fills me. My head still pounding from the accident. My heart rapidly beating begging me desperately to keep him.

We get to the elevator; Finn presses the button, and we wait for it to come. I'm fidgeting, I can't help it, so many emotions racing through me. An overwhelming sense of nausea looming. My nerves are on edge. "Calm down, darlin', or you'll draw attention to us." His voice is low but laced with concern. His thumb runs small circles on my hand, just like he used to. I avert my eyes from the action, knowing I can't keep him.

I suck in a deep breath when we finally enter an empty elevator, relief making me almost slump against the back of the elevator wall.

We slowly start to descend, but then stop at the fourth floor. Finn's tall, lean body stands stoically beside me. I keep my head down low, slowly lifting my lashes to look above me as I recognize the uniform of a security officer.

I quickly squeeze my eyes shut and gather the courage to go through with the plan I'd implemented in the hospital room. It's the only way, but it doesn't make it any easier. I take a step back from Finn and pretend to adjust my shoelace. When the elevator reaches the first floor, I slip my hand to the security officer's and pass him the note I wrote out in the room.

The note informs him that Finn is trying to get me to leave the hospital with him under duress. I know it's a shitty thing to do, and if I could keep him, I selfishly would. But I also know that's not an option, not even a small possibility. I only wish there was another way.

This is the only way I can shake him off and lose him before too much is revealed. There's too much at stake and I'd do anything to protect him and my family.

The elevator pings, and we both step forward together, walking out.

Then, as we near the entrance, three other security men walk toward us. "Sir, can I have a quick word?" One officer asks Finn. I step away from Finn and walk around him, he doesn't realize it yet, but I've become a good little thief while I've been away from him and he won't be retrieving his wallet from his pocket, to show the guys ID. It's sat in my hoodie pocket, it's my ticket home.

I don't dare glance back at Finn. I said goodbye to him in the hospital room. It killed me to stare deep into his blue eyes, knowing it would be the last time I'd see him, but wishing with all my heart it wasn't.

I'm pretty sure he saw the pain I felt, but he doesn't deserve the weight of that pain and I'm not prepared to share it with him.

I'll always protect the ones I love, even if they need protecting from me.

CHAPTER 3

2 **Weeks later.**

Finn

"What's that you're fidgeting with?" Oscar prompts with a sigh.

I'm sat thumbing the small scrap of paper that Angel had placed into my pocket in replace of my wallet. It's got one word on it, 'sorry.' Fucking sorry. Sorry for what? Stealing my wallet? Lying to me? Breaking my fucking heart? I wince at the pain I have in my chest every time I think of her. God damn it.

I shrug, nursing the same beer I've had for the past hour.

Oscar came up to sit in my apartment after Cal called him and told him to check on me. Apparently, my torture techniques have been 'off' just lately.

"Why do you think she left a sorry note?" I ask him vulnerably.

Oscar stares at me blankly. Fair enough, I'm asking the wrong brother. He doesn't get the whole emotion thing.

"Maybe she's sorry she had to leave?" he says quietly.

That surprises me. I thought he'd say she was sorry for stealing my wallet. I snap my head up to study him. "What makes you say that?"

"Well, she sounded pretty freaked out, right? And you're convinced she's hiding something?" I nod at what he's saying. He pushes his glasses up his nose. "Well, I think it's obvious. She didn't want to leave you, but felt she had no other choice."

I tilt my head in acknowledgment of his words. This is exactly my train of thought too, and it kills me inside to think she didn't trust me enough to tell me what the fuck is going on. To protect her.

I lick my lips with a newfound confidence. "That's what I'm thinking too. I mean, I've been going over it and over it in my fucking head," I tug at my hair in frustration, "and the more I think about it, the more I think she said goodbye to me in the hospital room." I exhale in annoyance with myself. Why the fuck didn't I do something then? Why didn't I realize?

Oscar sits straighter, "Well, I kind of took it upon myself to do a little research with the information you gave me..." his voice sounds unsure.

I bolt up on my sofa, "You did?"

"Yeah. I mean, you know what I'm like. It's kind of a challenge." Oscar acts like it's nothing, but I know it is. He's been looking into things for me. It's everything to me.

"What did you find?" My throat bobs in uncertainty.

"Okay, so Chad, I'm pretty sure it's a strip club named after the owner himself." I intake a sharp breath. A fucking strip club. Oscar ignores my internal meltdown and continues on, "I'm sure she probably knows the guy or works the bar?" He stares at me over his glasses, with a skeptical look.

Yeah, she best work the fucking bar, otherwise I'll spank her ass so badly she'll wish she only worked the fucking bar.

"Okay, anything else?" I spit out, pissed she might be showing my tits to someone else.

"Yeah, I located this Tyler dude as well." He turns the tablet to me and shows me his photo.

"Yeah, that's him." I confirm with confidence.

"Okay so, his names Tyler Reynalds. I've got his home address and I'm pretty convinced you'll find Angel there, too."

I smile, a big mega-watt fucking smile.

Yeah, I'm coming for ya Angel and I'm bringing you home, darlin'.

CHAPTER 4

Finn

I've been sitting solo at the small table, nursing a beer, watching the whole dynamic of the club. I've scanned every staff member and still no fucking sign of her. This is my third night in a row. If I don't find her here tonight, I'm going to the apartment address I have for her buddy, Ty.

I just wanted to get a feel for her work life dynamic before going in all guns blazing to an apartment I don't know for sure she lives in. I certainly don't want to add to any trouble she might already be in, so I've kept my distance from the apartment as directed by Oscar.

The music changes and the lights drop, ready for another dancer to come out and shake her tits at the crowd. To be fair, it's a busy night tonight for a weeknight, so the girls working will probably earn a shit ton of green in tips. I smile to myself, chewing on my toothpick. There could be worse places to spend the night.

The room falls seductively silent and the music blends into the background as I sit entranced by the dancer on stage. She's fucking hot. High black heels, lacy black lingerie and nothing else. My cock twitches in appreciation. I can't see her face, but her hair flows down her back in waves and the lights give a red tinge to it.

My heart suddenly beats faster. Please fuck, tell me it isn't her. Her back is to the crowd as she peels her black lacy bra off. My heart stops, my body stills. She seductively glances over her shoulder with heat in her eyes, and my fucking stomach plummets. Jesus, what the fuck have you done Angel? Green emeralds shine back at me.

I can't move a fucking muscle, so entranced by her provocative moves. Her leg slides up the pole, and she wraps it around the top, pulling herself up and sliding slowly down into the splits.

Her hair is covering her tits as she crawls forward, staring out directly toward the crowd, piercing them with those innocent greens. My girl's green eyes. My chest thumps rapidly. Mine.

She licks her top lip, that is painted in slut fucking red. My hard-on is throbbing against my jeans' zipper, causing me to wince. I will myself to move, but I'm stuck. I'm fucking paralyzed.

I hear high-pitched voices over at the left toward the bar, and quickly my eyes zone in on the commotion. A tall, thickly muscled guy is behind the bar, glaring toward the stage, his face contorted in rage, red with anger. It radiates from him, the pulse ticking in his thick neck.

A barmaid beside him seems to plead with him. Her face panicked. He spares her a glance and then he shoots off over the bar like a fucking rocket and runs toward the stage. I barely make it out of my seat before he's got Angel over his shoulder and marching off the stage to a chorus of laughs and boos. He kicks the 'Employee Only' door open, and through they go, disappearing.

I waste no time following after them.

Angel

I'm having an amazing time. I love dancing and stripping. It makes me feel in control and sexy as hell. It's also pretty damn good for getting some great tips at the end of the night.

I can feel someone's eyes locked onto me and the sensation of being watched so closely sends prickles down my spine. I try to shake off the feeling and concentrate on my routine.

I've just started crawling toward the crowd when I hear raised voices. I block them out. Security will deal with those jerks. I need to give it my best shot tonight, knowing Chad is out of town. It's the best way for me to make some funds quickly.

I'm just about to rise to my knees and push my tits together when I'm swooped up and thrown over a shoulder. What. The. Fuck?

A familiar scent surrounds me, "Chad?" He kicks the door open, anger radiating off of him.

Chad marches us down to his office and unlocks the door, before he abruptly drops me on the chair and goes to his bar, pouring himself a generous whiskey. He downs it and throws himself into his chair, breathing out to tamper his anger. He refuses to look at me.

Well, fuck him. I point toward the door. "What the fuck was that? What the hell is your problem?"

He scoffs, his angry eyes meeting mine. "You're kidding me, right? My problem? My fucking problem is you're meant to be a barmaid, not an exotic dancer, not a fucking stripper, not someone shaking their tits for a quick buck!"

I seethe, so pissed at his train of thought. How dare he? This is my life, my body. "You're a hypocrite Chad. I need the money, so made the call and decided to take the opportunity while I had it." I shrug and look down to inspect the nail I've chipped, hoping to give him the 'I don't give a shit what you think attitude.'

"You don't give a shit, do you? I'm doing this to protect you," his eyes plead with me to see sense.

"Bull shit, you're doing this to protect yourself. Some egotistical macho man bull shit that doesn't like me on the stage trying to earn myself good money, legally may I add!" I cross my arms like a petulant child.

Chad scoffs, "Legally? You're seriously pulling the legal card now, Chelsea? It wasn't that fucking long ago you were in a road collision after crashing a car you stole, for Christ's sake! And not just any car, a fucking police officer's son's car."

I roll my eyes. Seriously, if I had a dollar every time, he threw that one in my face. I wouldn't need to steal cars or strip, for that matter. "Mmm, I heard you the first, second, third, fucking hundredth time you brought that up, Chad. Give me a break. I need the money. I used my initiative, got up on the stage, and shook my tits. No big fucking deal." My voice rises beyond the room, eager for him to understand.

Chad breathes out, trying to regulate his temper before speaking to me again in a placid, patronizing tone. "Look sweetie, I'm only trying to help. If you need money, you've only got to ask. You're like family to me, I won't have you up on that stage for all the fucking perverts in the area to drool and jerk off over you. Do you hear me?" His voice sharpens again.

God, I could scream. This man infuriates me so much. "Like I've explained a thousand times. I don't want to ask you for money, Chad. I don't want to ask Tyler for money. I want to earn my own. Me, I need to do this. Me!" I point at myself.

His face turns solemn, his tone gentle. "I get that. Really, I do. But you've got to be smart with it Chels, you can't be fucking stealing cars, getting attention from God knows who on stage. You're meant to be flying under the radar, not getting more attention. Think about it. You've got people out there, quite literally, ready to kill you. You need to be a sensible girl."

His words hit me like a ton of bricks. He's right. Jesus. Why was he always fucking right? So stupid Chelsea. I stare down at my hands, feeling deflated. Swallowing hard, I admit, "You're right, I've been a dick."

"Look. Go put some clothes on, and you can be finished for the night. But first, come here and give us a hug." His soft tone wraps around my heart, reminding me I have people who care about me.

No matter how many bust ups and bad words me and Chad have had over the past few years, we could always hug it out and carry on. He's been incredibly supportive, him and Ty. We work. Our own little family, and I'm so thankful for that.

CHAPTER 5

Angel

After begrudgingly throwing on my clothes and slamming my locker door shut so hard it rattles, I push open the back exit door, completely disappointed and pissed at how the night turned out. I'd hoped to get some serious green, but instead I got another fucking lecture. At the thought, I roll my eyes. I know Chad means well, but Jesus was he overbearing sometimes. So, what if I want to shake my tits for a bit of cash? I grumble to myself.

Then, like always, I have a wave of guilt hit me like a ten-ton truck. He's right, of course. Fuck, he is right. I need to lie low. I've far too much at stake.

The cold air hits me, and I instantly tighten my leather jacket around my tank top. My bare legs shiver, making me wish I'd put on jeans instead of this skimpy little mini skirt. Great idea Chels. I shake my head at myself before drawing to a complete halt, my eyes scan in front of me. Suddenly, I'm frozen, my body goes rigid, and my heart skips a beat because there in front of me, leaning casually against a blacked-out SUV in the alleyway. With a toothpick hanging from his cocky mouth is Finn. My Finn. My heart hammers in my chest as emotion clogs my throat.

He throws his toothpick onto the ground, his angry eyes penetrating my body, making me shift back a step at the intensity.

Finn's fists clench and unclench beside him as he rakes his gaze wildly up and down my body. His face contorted with hostility, the veins in his neck protrude abnormally. My throat goes dry, making me lick my lips. Finn's eyes dart to them, then narrow at the action, then they flick up to meet my eyes, blazing with desire and, if I'm not mistaken, possessiveness.

The silent battleground we were both contained to was obliterated by me crossing my arms tightly under my chest and giving him a glaring, 'I don't give a shit attitude' look.

Finn sucks in a deep breath. Dropping his head down toward the ground, his chest heaving, his body visibly vibrating as if struggling to rein himself in, simmering with rage.

I take another step back, conscious of the wall behind me. His body doesn't miss my reaction to his movements. Finn's head darts up, and he glares at me from under his eyelashes, his face shadowed by the darkness surrounding us. I inhale a sharp deep breath, desperate for air, desperate to breathe again. My heart races wildly, causing my chest to vibrate.

Finn steps forward and I close my eyes at his reaction, darting them open when his deep voice echoes around us. He punctuates each word slowly, aggression rolling off his tongue. "What. In. The. Ever. Living. Fuck, are you playing at Angel?" His venomous tone catching me off guard, making me shudder like a naughty child.

He rushes toward me, not giving me a chance to move quickly enough, causing my whole-body to push harshly against the wall. Finn cages me in, his tall body towering over me, his fists tighten against the wall as he stares down at me.

His cologne floods my senses and I inhale him, loving his tall, hard body shadowing over me.

A tsunami of emotions washes over his handsome face. Anger. Jealousy. Possessiveness. Desire.

Then finally the worse, pity seeps through his eyes.

My stomach plummets and a wave of sickness rises. I push at his solid chest. "Don't fucking pity me, Finn. I wanted this. This is my choice!" I point my finger at my chest and raise my chin confidently. This is my choice. I choose to do this.

"You look like a fucking slut!" He spits out, his eyes meet mine, searching for a reaction.

My voice catches on a choked laugh, the surprise in his eyes evident when he almost stumbles back in shock, giving me the confidence to push further. "I enjoy doing it. All those men eye fucking me, knowing it's my choice and they can't have me." I grin knowingly at him.

His chest vibrates, his jaw clenches tight, and his nostrils flare. He takes another step toward me, backing me back up against the wall once again.

Finn sneers down at me, then spins me around, grabbing my hips with bruising force. "You look like a slut and enjoy it?" His breath whispers in my ear. "Well, guess what? I'm going to treat you like one."

My thighs clench involuntarily at his dirty words. I gasp out loud when his icy hand moves between my thighs.

He sucks in a breath and struggles to say the words, choking on them as he struggles to get them out. "Fucking Jesus. No panties? No fucking panties?" He tilts his head beside my ear in question, his breath whispering through my hair. I gently shake my head in response to his question.

His fingers separate my folds, already swollen and wet from arousal. I cringe at my desperate response to him, then instantly find myself moaning when he presses one lone finger to my clit. "Finn…" escapes me with a breathy moan as he strokes me back and forth. My heart races and heat rises up my chest with each swipe of his finger.

"Dancing fucking topless?" He grits out as he shoves two fingers brutally into my pussy without warning, pumping them in and out. In and out. "You have such a wet fucking pussy, Angel. Is this from dancing? Dancing like a mother fucking slut?" His voice oozes disgust. "You're my fucking slut, Angel." He nips at the flesh on my neck, causing me to flinch. "Ya hear me? My dirty Angel." He pumps more aggressively, causing me to stand on my tiptoes. "Mine!" His hand withdraws fast. I sink to my feet in both relief and disappointment.

His belt buckle clangs. I peer over my shoulder to see Finn stroking his cock. His bold blue eyes meet mine, taunting and hate-filled. "Fucking slut," he rolls the words from his tongue. His hands push my skirt up over my ass, leaving me completely exposed to him. He raises his hand and smacks my ass cheek hard, causing me to stifle a whimper.

Finn pushes his body against mine, crushing me against the wall, giving me no time to think before he plunges into my pussy, using one hand to grip the back of my neck and push my head harshly against the wall while the other tightens on my hip. His cock pounds into me without giving me the benefit of accommodating him first. I wince at the stretch caused by his cock. The feel of him filling me whole.

Finn works his hips back and forth against me, his heavy balls hitting against me with vigor. The pounding motion making my cheek graze the wall, scraping up and down. Fuck, that hurts in a good way.

The overloading sensations of Finn brutally taking me, causes my body to become putty in his expert hands. Letting him use me desperately for his anger and release, the realization shamelessly turning me on. My clit throbs and aches, begging for his touch.

Finn grits his teeth. "Sweet fucking Jesus, Angel. Fucking

Jesus. Ain't ever letting you go, darlin'. Ain't ever." His words flow through me, warming my craving heart. My pussy clutches his cock on his words. "Fuck. Fuck. Fucking…" he chants, nearing his orgasm, his mouth falling open slightly beside my face.

The thought of him coming inside me knocks me sideways. My body goes rigid. Finn reacts instantly, slowing down to an almost complete stop. Desperately, I rush the words out desperately, "Finn. Stop. I'm not on birth control." I swallow hard in a panic, my heart pounding. "Stop. Please take… take my ass. I'm not on birth control." His body comes to a complete stop, as if to obey my request, before he tightens his hold on me and rams himself deeper and deeper into me. Oh shit, a sense of determination behind his movements.

Finn

Her panic-stricken words chant inside my head as I ram my cock into her with wild abandonment. "Please take… take my ass. I'm not on birth control." The anger inside me boiling to a peak. Take her ass? Her fucking ass? I never took her ass! Never. My need grows for her while chanting the words. "Not on birth control." Sweet fucking Jesus, I almost lost it at that. She isn't on birth control. Well, she ain't ever leaving me. She will leave this shit hole tonight with a permanent piece of me inside her. Growing, ensuring she's mine.

I come, I come so fucking hard I roar, my eyes seeing stars. My legs wobble as my cum floods my girl's pussy, flooding her bare womb. "Oh, fuck, Angel. Holy…" I bite into her exposed neck, tugging on the skin. Her pussy squeezes every drop of cum from my tender cock, milking it while she screeches in ecstasy, sending a final unexpected spurt from my spent dick. I've never come so hard in my entire life.

We pant in unison, coming down from the euphoric high. I nuzzle into her neck and place a gentle kiss on the bite mark, breathing in her scent. Fucking strawberries.

Angel's body slinks against mine as she moves her head to the side to give me better access to her neck. "Fuck, I missed you, darlin'," I admit, my chest still rising and falling rapidly. I hold her eyes with my own, hoping she can see the truth behind my words.

My cock falls from her pussy, completely forgotten about. My eyes glance down her body, her juices drip down the inside of her thigh, and Angel's body freezes in response, causing me to quickly step back, tuck myself in, and zip up. Angel tugs down her skirt aggressively before spinning on her heels and launching herself at me.

Her fists hammer at my chest as I remain stoically still during her little outburst, caught completely off guard. "You bastard! You mother fucking bastard, Finn! Oh, my god, you came inside me! I'm not on birth control, you prick. Did you not hear me? Did you?" She steps back and stares up at me, my eyes trained on her delicate features contorted with rage. I smirk at her and shrug carelessly.

Angel's mouth drops open, her eyes wide. "Are you insane? Oh, my god. Are you even clean? Please tell me you're clean, right?"

My smirk disappears and transforms into anger. How fucking dare she? I point toward the car, "Get your ass in the mother fucking car now Angel before I drag you in it!" I spit the words out at her. She doesn't move an inch. The rage in her face dissipated now, taking over with shock. I take a step toward her, and she instantly glances at the car, then down the sidewalk before looking back at me. I shake my head with a small smile on my lips. No way, darlin', no way are you running from me again.

Angel sighs heavily, admitting defeat. Her shoulders slump and I can't help but feel triumphant at the fact. She moves toward the car, throwing her bag into the footwell before climbing in. I rush around to the driver's side and get in the car, her scent already consuming the interior. Once again, my cock twitches to life.

I start the engine and pull out of the alleyway. We sit in silence as I drive. With Angel staring out of the passenger window, her whole-body turned away from me. Pissing me off.

I scan her out of the corner of my eye, her body rigid, her hands clasped nervously in her lap. I brush a frustrated hand through my hair before turning to her again. "I'm clean. Okay?"

Her body sags and she turns her head to face me, a lone tear trailing down her beautiful face. Fuck, the sight of that one tear hits me in the gut. Her bottom lip quivers vulnerably, making me feel like a complete prick.

I glance at the road and then back at Angel. "You… you didn't use protection, Finn," her words catch on her throat, her eyes searching mine for an apology.

But she thought wrong because with her words, anger fills my veins. "I like the thought of my cum dripping out of your pussy." I shrug and turn my eyes back to the road. My smirk firmly in place.

Angel sits forward, and I don't pay her any attention. "You fucking came inside me, Finn! I told you I wasn't on birth control. You came in me!" She screeches like a banshee.

I dart my eyes toward her, my voice stern. "Fucking heard you the first time, Angel. Now sit back and shut the fuck up like a good girl." I curl my lip into a smile, infuriating her even more. Her eyebrows reach her hairline, her mouth opens and closes. What I'd give to stick my tongue in there right now and show her how much she means to me. The thought makes my dick swell. I blatantly adjust myself, then dart my eyes up at Angel, her eyes tracking the movement. She shakes her head, mortified. "You're fucking insane, Finn. Insane!"

I laugh. "You've no fucking idea, darlin'." No idea at all.

Checking the GPS, I see we're five minutes from Angel's apartment. My heart speeds up at the thought of her leaving the car. I clumsily reach down to the cup holder and take the packet of cigarettes out, fumbling to light it but desperate for a taste to take the edge away. I haven't had a cigarette in over 8 years. I can sense Angel watching me, but I choose to ignore her.

Lighting the cigarette, I inhale deeply; fuck how I've missed this.

Angel's voice is low, a soft delicate whisper. "I don't like you smoking, Finn." My fingers freeze before reaching my mouth again.

She always used to tell me she hated me smoking. They reminded her of her mother and the men that used to visit her. She's the reason I gave them up in the first place. Now

47

she's the reason I've fucking started again. I shake my head at the realization. Press my window button and launch the cigarette, then the whole packet out the window.

Angel gasps. "You just threw your cancer sticks out the window?"

I lift a shoulder and scan her face for seriousness. Yeah, she's serious. I choke on a laugh. Her Angel's mortified face watches me. "What's so fucking funny, Finn?"

I glare at her. She's serious all right. "You stole my wallet, Angel. Oh, and let's not forget the fucking car you crashed. Pretty sure you beat me on the playing good citizen count."

Her eyes narrow on me before she quickly changes the subject. "How the hell do you know where I live?" Her eyes frantically searching out the windows almost as if only now realizing we're on her street. "Finn. How do you know where I live?" Her voice trembles. "Who else knows Finn?" Her voice now pleading, her chest rising and falling, her small body begins to shake.

I turn the car off outside her apartment building and lean over the center console. "Darlin', chill the fuck out. Nobody knows, just me and Oscar." Her eyes search mine questioningly. Does she not believe me? I squeeze her hands and draw them up toward my chest, laying them over my heart. Slowly her breathing regulates, her eyes not leaving my chest, our hands.

Angel's throat bobs slowly. "I can't do this Finn," she pulls away abruptly, not giving me a chance to stop her. I deflate as I watch her open her door and rush out of the car toward her building.

I quickly push the window button down and deepen my voice to make sure she knows how serious I am. "You don't have a choice anymore, Angel. You're mine and I'm never letting you go. Never!" Her shoulders tighten at my words, and she pushes through the door, ignoring me.

Absolutely no choice. She might have taken away my choice in the past, but now?

Now I'm taking away hers.

CHAPTER 6

Finn

It killed me staying away from her last night. I called Oscar on a burner phone to give him an update and to also ask him for some advice. He suggested leaving her overnight, giving her a bit of space. I haven't fucking slept worrying she's going to do a runner on me. I was tempted to sleep in the car outside her apartment just to make sure she didn't leave, but Oscar reassured me he was watching on the security cameras he's managed to access surrounding her apartment block.

I switch the car engine off and peer up at the apartment building. It's still early and the blinds are closed. I grab the box of doughnuts I picked up for breakfast and exit the car to make my way inside.

The apartment block is similar to the one Angel grew up in, dank, scruffy, and poor. The elevator is broken and there's graffiti covering the walls, the stairwell stinks of stale piss. I grimace. Pissed that my girl is living in such a shit hole, what the hell is she thinking?

What the fuck happened to her happy marriage on the West Coast? Does she have an abusive ex or something? And that's why she changed her name? The whole thing doesn't make sense, but it's eerily similar to both my brother's women's experiences, both also hiding from their pasts. So many fucking secrets and lies.

Well, Angel is done hiding. I won't accept it, no fucking way.

I bang on the door with my fist, not caring if I scare her shitless or wake up the junkie neighbors. I can hear giggling behind the door and the scuffle of feet. My heart sinks and my spine straightens with anger. How dare she fucking giggle when I spent the entire night freaking out? And just who the hell is she giggling with? Has she got a man in there?

The door opens slowly, and my eyes are drawn down to a little girl. My heart stills and my breath catches because in the doorway is a sweet, innocent little replica of Angel. A petite little princess with long blonde hair, a cute little face with rosy cheeks.

Where Angel has piercing green eyes like emeralds, this little princess has dark eyes, bordering on black.

She tilts her head from side to side, assessing me as much as I am her. "You brought doughnuts?" Her cute little voice asks as she points to the doughnut box, breaking me out of my trance.

I swallow hard, still in shock, my mouth opens but the words don't come out.

"Who's at the door, Charlie?" A familiar guy coos as his footsteps approach the entrance. He pulls open the door and his eyes widen before he chokes on a laugh. "Well, well, well, Finn-fitty is in the house!" He throws his arms up in the air with a gleeful shriek, causing the little princess to giggle and jump up and down like an adorable puppy.

I scan the dude up and down, still in shock. Tyler is now in a rainbow-colored tutu that clearly matches little Charlie's. His bare legs are on full display and they both have Dr. Martens boots on, both wearing t-shirts with a diamanté tiara on the front, and both have a sparkly tiara on their heads. Tyler holds a wand with a shiny star on the top.

Tyler's cocky smile lights up his entire face, clearly enjoying my shocked reaction.

It feels like some twilight light zone shit is going on, that's for sure. I glance down the corridor before bringing my eyes back to meet Tyler's. Are other people seeing this?

His smile broadens, "Finn-fitty brought doughnuts!" The little princess declares with glee in her cute voice.

Tyler's eyebrows shoot up. "He did?" Charlie nods, staring up at the dude in awe. "Is Finn-fitty going to come in or is he going to stand in the hallway looking like a fish all day?" He asks mockingly before exaggerating opening and closing his mouth, making Charlie giggle and gaze up at me with pleading eyes.

Jesus, she's adorable, just like her mama. I swallow the pain away. The thought that Angel had a little girl without me. "Jesus," I mutter to myself as I scrub a hand through my hair, my palms sweating with discomfort.

"Ah-oh! You said a swear! He said a swear, Ty!" Charlie's eyes bug out and dart from mine to Tyler's for confirmation.

Tyler pouts his lips and puts his hands on his hips playfully. "He did, didn't he? Get the jar, Charlie," he nods at her with all seriousness, and she pushes past him with haste, disappearing into the apartment.

Tyler watches me with scrutinizing eyes drilling into my own, his playful voice turning serious as he blocks my entrance with an arm across the doorway. "So, are you here to stay?"

I don't give him time to question my response. "I'm not going any fucking where." He nods in approval and smiles to himself as if I passed some sort of hidden test.

Tyler moves away from the door and spreads his arm out with a sweeping motion for me to enter.

Angel

I've barely slept all night. Even after taking my medication, I couldn't switch off. Thank God Tyler was home to get up with Charlie.

I groan as I skulk out of bed sluggishly and go into the ensuite.

Washing my face with the ice-cold water to wake me up. My eyes catch on the mirror, and I take a deeper look at myself. Hating the reflection of the woman staring back at me. My throat clogs with emotion. Finn must have barely recognized me with the transformation I've undertaken in the last eight years. My once golden locks are now hidden behind cherry red hair and my left arm is almost completely covered in tattoos. I close my eyes, willing away the image of the innocent teen I once was. Naïve and so very stupid, so trusting, I shake my head in shame at myself. My heart speeds up, panic building as I clutch the sink to ground myself. But the sweet giggle of my little girl pulls me back, saves me.

My new self.

I raise my head and shake away the insecurities of my past and deal with the present. Walking out of my bedroom to the smell of coffee and toast, Charlie's excitable voice fills the open plan living area.

My eyes draw up instantly to the doorway like a magnet locking onto him. Stepping into the apartment is Finn. His face pale and uncertain, his nervous gaze meeting mine. Fuck, he's gorgeous. My heart beats faster, but this time out of excitement. His dark hair is longer than it used to be, the heavy locks causing his waves to dissipate, his hair straighter now but messy. It suits him; I imagine running my hands through it, like I used to. His soft blue eyes search mine vulnerably, as if waiting for me to reject him. My own eyes shoot over toward Charlie, unsure if Finn has met her yet. My eyes quickly go back to Finn's in a panic. A small, tight smile graces his handsome face, letting me know he's seen her. My shoulders and head sag in both relief and defeat. I squeeze my eyes closed before reopening them and lifting my head.

"Finn-fitty said a swear!" Charlie declares, rushing over to him with her plastic swear jar. I wince at my little girl carrying a huge jar half-filled in dollars over toward Finn. He chuckles uncomfortably at her, before pulling out his wallet from his back pocket and throwing in a couple of dollars. Charlie's face lights up with glee.

"You know you could just put ten dollars in that buys you the week," she cheekily grins up at him proudly. "My mom has to do that. She has a real potty mouth."

Finn's accusing eyes dart to mine. "She does, huh?" They narrow on me, making me shift uncomfortably from foot to foot. Finn never did like me swearing. He liked me to be a good girl. Finn proceeds to put ten dollars in the jar. Charlie happily skips away, her blonde hair flowing behind her. Finn's eyes don't leave mine. Watching, scrutinizing.

I glance down at myself, tugging on my tank top as if trying to extend it past my bare waistline. Tyler clears his throat. "Coffee?" My eyes dart to his and I glare at him accusingly, my jaw tightening in annoyance. I explained to him about what had happened at the club last night and Tyler already knows all about my past, so he's well aware who Finn is and, more importantly, he's well aware of why he needs to be kept at arm's length. No matter how much I'd like him to be close. Need him to be close.

"He brought doughnuts!" Tyler points toward Finn. Who proceeds to hold the doughnut box up like a trophy. As if that makes everything okay. I roll my eyes at Tyler and shake my head nervously, causing Tyler to chuckle. "Chill out Chels, he's here for the long-haul, aren't you Finn-fitty?" Tyler's eyebrows do a little dance in Finn's direction.

My eyes meet Finn's intense stare, his tone dark, sending shivers down my spine. "She knows I am. Don't you, Angel?"

I shift my eyes away and ignore him. Walking over to the living room chair, I plonk myself down and draw my legs up to my chest. My mind overriding with thoughts and problems, I clutch my head in frustration, tugging at my hair.

I can vaguely hear Tyler talking to Finn and Charlie, I can hear him busying himself in the kitchen area and then I hear Finn's footsteps approaching, the squeak of his boots on the floor. He sits down on the couch opposite me. "Talk to me, Angel." His voice is as soft as a whisper. I shake my head, leaving it buried in my hands, making him sigh in frustration.

"Mommy, did you pay for my camping trip? Holly says it's amazing and school said you didn't pay it yet. It's on Tuesday and I really want to go; I didn't get to last year and Holly said there's horse riding too." My head pops up at Charlie's words, meeting her doughnut clad smile, my heart melting. "Did you pay now?" She sits down next to Finn, watching me, her fingers pulling the doughnut apart before nonchalantly munching on the pieces. I swallow thickly and move my eyes away from her, knowing I'm going to break my little girl's heart. I open my mouth, but Finn's voice stills me.

"Yeah, your mama told me all about your trip, Charlie. It sounds incredible, princess. In fact, that's why I called round. I owed your Mommy some money, and I was here to give it to her; now how much was that trip of yours?" He raises an eyebrow in question at my wide-eyed daughter.

I sit gob smacked at Finn. Watching the interaction with Charlie, her eyes alight with pure joy, "It was fifteen hundred dollars wasn't it, Mommy? But you paid six hundred already, right?" I wince at Charlie's words. The realization that I didn't manage to pay for the trip, again.

"So you need nine hundred dollars then, princess, right?" Charlie nods unknowingly at Finn's words. "Here we go." Finn pulls the wad of cash out of his wallet, and I glance away, unable to watch the transaction between my daughter and my ex.

Charlie throws herself at Finn, sending him barreling backward against the couch. His deep chuckle causing me to involuntarily smile at their cute interaction. "Princess, you're getting doughnut stuck in your hair." He smiles back at her.

Charlie pulls away, grinning, before licking her sticky fingers into her mouth to clean them. "I'll go wash them up," she nods to herself before disappearing down the hallway.

I reluctantly meet Finn's eyes. "You need cash? That why you were dancing last night?" His voice turns low as he moves forward, leaning his elbows on his knees so he's level with me. His eyes scan over my face for answers. "That why you stole the car?" He quizzes.

I nod at him without looking in his direction. I chew the skin from the side of my nail anxiously. Finn roughly brushes a hand through his hair, his voice cold and deep. "Jesus, Angel."

Tyler walks into the living area and thankfully breaks the intensity between us. "I told her I'd give her the cash. She didn't have to get herself into shit. But noooo, she wants to do it herself. On some dumb, 'I don't need help' bullshit thing she's got going on." Tyler air quotes the words, causing my eyes to roll.

Finn watches Tyler with admiration. "I'm gonna go get ready. Guess Charlie's going to need some hiking boots now, huh?" Tyler smiles at me. I move to open my mouth but close it when he holds his hand up and starts talking again. "Look, I told you I'd get her a few bits for her birthday and so I'll get her the boots. I'll put the money in the bank for you, too. Pay for the trip now on your phone. I just transferred enough funds." He smiles at me pointedly and I just nod with a tight smile in agreement. Once again, feeling like a total failure.

The door down the corridor closes and Finn moves toward me slowly but pulls back quickly when Charlie descends on us like a whirlwind. Whatever he was going to say is now gone and I couldn't be more grateful for Charlie's intrusion.

"I'm making a list. Uncle Ty said he's getting me everything I need for camping. Isn't that cool? It's for my birthday, but I get them early, right?" She looks at me for confirmation.

"Yeah, sweetheart, you do." I smile tightly at her.

"When's your birthday, princess?" Finn asks as he watches her write in her notepad.

"Next month. The twelfth and I'm going to be eight!" She virtually screams with glee, her face lighting up in delight.

CHAPTER 7

Finn

"Next month. The twelfth and I'm going to be eight!" Charlie's words echo around in my head as I try to make sense of them. Just under nine years ago, Angel disappeared out of my life. I'm twenty six now and not a day has gone by when I haven't thought about her and what we could have been. I scan Angel for some sort of reaction. Nothing. Her eyes were completely besotted with Charlie, oblivious to my inner turmoil.

The dates work over in my mind. Is Charlie mine? Turning myself toward Charlie, my hands tremble as I take her in again. Her nose has the same cute scattering of freckles as Angel's. Her eyes don't resemble either of us. Honestly? I don't even know what the fuck I'm looking for. Just something that tells me she's mine. God, anything.

Anger starts boiling in my veins. Anger at the lies and deceit behind Angel's actions.

Before I know what's happening, Angel is kissing Charlie goodbye and she and Tyler leave the apartment in matching denim jackets.

The silence between me and Angel was palpable.

My fists clench and unclench at my sides. I stare venomously into Angel's eyes. She sucks in a breath at what I can only imagine, the murderous expression on my face. "She's almost eight?" I ask, but obviously already know the answer.

Angel nods solemnly, struggling to meet my stare. I hold her eyes. "She mine?" My heart pounds aggressively against my chest. My palms are sweating. Did she do this to me? Keep me from my child?

Angel jolts at my words, then pales. Her lip quivers, she licks her bottom lip with a swipe of her tongue. Taking far too long to answer. "Is. She. Fucking. Mine. Angel?" I punctuate the words, getting louder with each one.

Her voice breaks as she shakes her head with a tremble. "No."

My body jolts at her words. Jesus. I can't breathe.

I wasn't expecting that answer. My heart stops in my chest and a raw aching pain takes over, my struggle to get my words out evident.

"You cheated? You fucking cheated on me while I was in Iraq? While I was getting us a better life. You cheated?" My voice wavers with disappointment and dread, my heart pounding achingly fast. I scrub my hand through my hair. How could she do this to me? To us?

Angel's body goes rigid, her face turns thunderous. "Get the fuck out, Finn! Now!" She stands and points toward the door. I ignore her. She swallows thickly, "You don't get to come in here and accuse me of shit like that. How fucking dare you?!" Tears stream down her face as I watch her chest rise and fall.

I grit my teeth, determined not to relent. Determined not to let her tears affect me. I stare up at her, pointing my finger at her aggressively. "You disappeared over eight years ago, Angel. Eight fucking years ago when I went in the forces for us. For a better life for us!" I spit the words out. "You left me

59

for some fucker on the west coast? While I was serving in fucking Iraq?" I struggle to catch my breath. "My brother fucking died, and you didn't even show your face," she winces when I say it. She knew Keenan. She knew him fucking well and still not a peep from her, nothing. Disappeared off the face of the fucking earth.

"I know he did. I'm so sorry, Finn." She stumbles and holds onto the couch, but I ignore her. Determined to get my words out, the anger built over the years.

I shake my head venomously. "You weren't that sorry, Angel. You didn't even send a card. A fucking text. You were like a daughter to my Ma! She needed you! I fucking needed you!" I scream at her, digging my finger into my own chest.

Her pale face is covered in tears, dripping down her cheeks. Clutching her head, "I... I couldn't. You don't understand. I couldn't!" she pleas desperately, but I ignore her and carry on with my tirade.

"You don't get to cry now, Angel. You don't have my fucking forgiveness. Do you know how much I fucking hated you? Leaving me like that?" I reach out and grab her wrist, pulling her toward me, the brutality of the force making her stumble to the floor on all fours. She pulls herself up on her knees and the image of her there in front of me, trembling with tears streaking down her beautiful face, causes my cock to twitch. Like the twisted son of a bitch I am, I need her. Now.

A sick sense of satisfaction of her in a vulnerable state at my will. My heart races. "Get up!" I spit out in disgust as I sneer down at her. She puts her palm on my knee to pull herself up and I use the opportunity to drag her onto my lap, making her small frame straddle me.

I gulp deeply, blood flowing thickly through my veins at the gorgeous sight before me. I whip my hand out to wrap it around her throat, squeezing gently at her pulse points.

Angel's pupils dilate when I press on her throat. My cock

twitches. My girl is fucking dirty. I use my other hand and wrap her cherry locks around it, tugging on them tightly. A gasp leaves her mouth. I can feel the pre-cum oozing out of my cock because of her own excitable state. I squeeze my eyes closed for a second to rein in my already impending release.

I almost choke on the words. "Take my cock out." I'll fucking show her what she does to me.

Angel wastes no time to think, desperate girl. I lick my lips approvingly, watching her as she unbuckles my jeans with trembling hands. Her dainty fingers working the buttons frantically. She slips her hand into my boxers, and I hiss and buck my hips the moment her silky palm touches my cock. "Fuck, that feels good." I close my eyes at the sensation. Over eight fucking years since her touch. I open my eyes, determined to watch everything she does to me.

Angel's mouth drops open and I feel her clench between her thighs. Working together, I push her little sleep shorts to the side, the stickiness to them clear of her arousal. With my free hand, I drag my fingers through her dripping folds, rubbing gently over her little bud of nerves. Another gasp leaves her mouth, causing her to lift herself up and push my bare cock toward her entrance. The thought of fucking her raw again making an aggressive desire and determination flood my veins. She drops her little pussy down on my cock, causing my eyes to roll at the tightness. Fuck, that's incredible. I take my hand from her throat to still her movement, gripping her hip to stop her moving.

Her eyes meet mine in question. "Open." I demand in a sharp tone. I hold up the fingers that were playing with her pussy. "Open!" I snap again.

She opens her mouth like a good girl. "Suck." I push two fingers into her mouth, and she sucks them, her wet tongue swirling around the edges. I can feel her pussy clenching around my cock, and I can't take it anymore. Using my hips, I drive up into her. Her arm darts out to grip onto my shoulder, her fist twisting at my t-shirt, to steady herself.

"Oh god, Finn. Oh, fuck!" She cries out on a breathy groan.

I thrust into her relentlessly, fucking that little pussy hard, her tits bounce in my face. Angel's nails catch my neck and I hiss at the sensation of my little wildcat. My dirty Angel. My cock channels in and out of her soft pussy vigorously. Every now and again, I grind my hips sideways, causing her pussy to flutter.

Her moans and the sensation of her pussy walls squeezing me make my balls tingle. Fuck, I'm going to come. "Fucking come, Angel. Come all over my cock, darlin'." I ruthlessly demand while hammering into her.

Her pussy spasms and her mouth drops open in a squeal. She throws her head back and I can feel her soft hair brush against my balls.

"Fuck, Angel. Holy fuuckkk!" I grit out through clenched teeth as my orgasm consumes me. I drop my head forward, watching her tits rise and fall as my cum pumps into her pussy. Pump after pump, the satisfaction overwhelming.

I drop my face into her chest and kiss the top of her tits. Angel clutches me against her chest, her heart hammering ruthlessly against my face. Her voice a soft, vulnerable whisper. "I didn't cheat Finn, I swear it." I only realize now what she's doing. She's clutching my face to her heart instead of my hand. I squeeze my eyes closed, willing her words to be true, but the evidence proving otherwise. Lifting my hand and placing them over the top of hers, holding my face securely against her beating heart. I wish it was true. I wish she hadn't taken this from me.

Angel

We sit frozen together on the couch, neither one of us wanting to move. My breathing steadies against Finn's head, his palms still securely pressed against my own.

I can feel Finn deflating inside of me, his cum trickling down the inside of my thighs. Even so, I make no move. I've wanted him like this for as long as I can remember now. I've dreamed of this moment and now he's finally here. Squeezing my eyes shut, I take a deep breath of his scent, inhaling in his cologne and the musky smell of his leather jacket. The nostalgia of him is overwhelming. He's finally here. My only wish is to keep him. My breath hitches, a lump catching in my throat.

"Shh, it's okay darlin'. It's okay." Finn soothes, moving his hands and drawing circles on my thighs. "Gonna have to move, darlin'. My cocks slipping out," he chuckles against my breasts, making them jiggle. "Fuck, your tits are hot, darlin'."

I lean down and kiss his hair; his hands squeeze my thighs reassuringly tighter.

Finn's arms band around my ass, and he pulls us up, carrying me toward the hallway. I nuzzle into his neck as he carries me like a koala. "Which one's your room?"

"Second on the right." I nod down the hallway.

Finn strides into my room. Kicking the door behind him, he scans the room before his eyes locate the small bathroom. I squeeze myself to stop his cock from slipping out, causing Finn to laugh. "You're making me hard again, darlin'." He's not even joking. I can feel him filling me again.

Finn turns on the light and spins around in the bathroom, dropping my ass onto the sink countertop. He slowly takes a step back, disconnecting us. Finn's eyes not leaving my pussy, his pupils dilate when he sees his cum dripping out of me. He licks his lips, and his throat works harshly. "Fuck that's hot, Angel." His eyes flick back up to meet mine, filled with lust.

In a split second, he tugs down my sleep shorts and drops them to the floor, giving him the perfect view of my bare pussy, oozing his seed.

His hands grip my thighs to hold me open to him, then he uses one hand to scoop up his cum. He pushes his fingers inside me, then sweeps his fingers up to gather more, repeating the action.

"Finn?" I ask in question.

His eyes dart away from my pussy, an annoyed gleam in his eyes. "Open," he demands. I take a second too long to realize what he means; he grips my thigh tighter in annoyance. Then I open my mouth and welcome his fingers. Finn's eyes light up with unmistakable want. I whimper as he thrusts his fingers in and out of my mouth. The scent of his cum and the salty taste making my pussy contract with need.

"Fuckin Jesus, Angel. So damn hot. God damn dirty Angel." Finn steps closer, his once semi-hard cock now back to full mast. His hand leaves my thigh, and he tugs on his length, the motion matching that of his fingers entering my open mouth. "Lick 'em darlin', lick 'em clean." He chants as he begins fucking his hand. I open my legs wider on the counter and quickly move my hand down to circle my needy clit. My mouth dropping open the moment my fingers touch my engorged bud.

Finn's head ducks down to watch, his eyes in awe. His mouth open and his pupils heavy, he rubs the tip of his cock up and down my slit. "Fuckin', Jesus." He licks his lips appreciatively. The sensation of the head of his cock violently stroking my clit makes me moan in desperation.

"Finn…" the needy words tumble out of my mouth.

His eyes dart up to meet mine, then they drop to my chest, and he nods his head at my breasts. Without him having to say a word, I drop the straps of my cami top, and my heavy breasts fall out. "Holy shit!" Finn's mouth descends on my pierced nipple, sucking it into his mouth while ferociously rubbing his cock against my pussy.

His hot, wet tongue toying with my piercing. Motioning between sucking, licking and tugging. Sending my sensations into overload.

"Oh god, Finn. Oh!" My hand works fast, rubbing my clit harder. I can feel my orgasm on the brink of exploding. Finn must sense this, too. He bites my breast and sucks hard, his tongue sweeping around the hardened bud.

His long guttural groan causes me to explode as he rams his cock into me just in time for it to expand and pump his thick cum inside me. His hips work vigorously, "FUCK! FUCK!" He chants between his mouth attacking my breast, his other hand now squeezing and kneading the other.

Finally, he draws his head up and his mouth meets mine in a long, passionate kiss. Our tongues entwine and my hands grip his hair, pulling him tighter, closer to me.

Finn reluctantly pulls back, our breaths rapid. He rests his forehead against mine, our eyes meeting and my heart telling me to keep him. He gives me a simple nod, almost like he heard my thoughts, followed up by a sweet, delicate kiss on my lips.

CHAPTER 8

Finn

After washing Angel in the shower, careful not to wash away my cum from inside her sweet pussy, I've left her in the bathroom drying her hair. It took me fucking ages to wash her hair in that strawberry stuff that makes my cock so hard. Now I'm walking around her room looking for clues to what I don't know. But I have a raging boner thanks to the strawberry shampoo, I know that.

I tighten the towel on my hip to secure my cock in place and then I scan the room.

A crisp, clean, white duvet covered double bed fills almost the entire room. Odd garments are scattered around the floor. A picture frame with Angel and Charlie sits beside her bed, Charlie's adorable smile staring up at her mama in awe. My heart swells at my two girls. I swallow the lump in my throat and move to her bedside table and open the drawer clumsily.

I rattle around the items, nothing of interest. A book about parenting, few pens, tissues. Fuck all, really.

I move toward her closet.

Clothes are crammed on a rail, shoes littering the floor. Jesus, it's a shit tip. I shake my head. She's going to love her walk-in closet at my apartment. Pride fills me at the thought of being able to provide for my girls.

A cardboard box up on the top shelf draws my attention. I grab it and place it on the bed. Glancing over my shoulder to make sure Angel is still occupied, I listen for her. I can hear the dryer still working, so I open the box. Swallowing thickly with worry at what I'm going to find. Answers?

Photos, a shit ton of photos.

Mainly of Charlie at various stages in her life. I feel almost sick looking through them, a hollow feeling of disappointment and guilt, guilt for not being her daddy. I rub the pain in my heart, my body shaking, overtly conscious of me not being her daddy.

I want to kill whoever the fuck he is for cheating me out of what is mine. My jaw pops painfully in aggravation.

A couple more photos show Charlie with Chad and Tyler. I clench my teeth. Is Chad her dad? Jealousy curses through my veins, my temple throbs. I almost rip the photo in my clenched fist. I throw it back down in the box and drop the lid on it. Essentially closing the thoughts rapidly building inside me.

I place the box back on the shelf and move on to her dresser. Pulling open drawer after drawer and finding fuck all, just more clothes.

I reach the bottom drawer and curse out loud when I see what's in there. "Jesus Christ, Angel, fuck." A white lacy teddy dress is folded neatly on the top. I push it aside and my body stops-dead at the remaining contents.

A drawer full of fucking sex toys. I flick my eyes to the bathroom in question, then back at the drawer, pushing the contents around before my temper flares and I rip the drawer off of the runner and unload the whole fucking thing onto Angel's bed.

I step back from the bed in shock and mortification. A dildo, a pile of vibrators, lube, butt plugs, a fucking cock ring?

I'm seething. Absolutely fucking livid. She's been doing this shit with other guys? What the hell?

Handcuffs, a gag, condoms, silky rope shit, I rummage through the stash. Little G-strings, some sort of flogger or cane? What. The. Ever. Living. Fuck? I glare at the bathroom door accusingly. Is she into this shit? Is this what she likes now? My nostrils flare and I struggle to rein in my breathing. Well, it all stops now. The only thing she needs is me.

The hairdryer stops, and I hear the clink of her hairbrush being put down. My senses are hyperaware of her movements.

I stand with my arms crossed over my chest in front of me. Waiting with simmering rage at the latest enlightenment. My girl has turned into a fucking sexual deviant.

Angel opens the door and walks into the room, her eyes automatically meeting mine before her eyebrows furrow in confusion at my expression before darting around the room searching for an explanation before finally landing on the bed. Her shoulders tense.

"What. In. The. Ever. Living. Fuck. Is. That?" I punctuate each word with a sneering tone and point aggressively toward the pile of sex fiends on the bed.

Angel sighs, causing her shoulders to sag before giving me more fucking attitude. "Toys Finn, they're toys." She shrugs it off as if it's nothing. Absolutely fucking nothing. Like she hasn't converted into some sort of living sex doll.

I suck in a shocked breath, my mouth dropping open. "Fucking toys? Legos are fucking toys!"

She bites her lip to stifle a giggle. My eyes bug out at her audacity. "Adult toys, Finn." She clarifies with a playful twinkle in her eyes. She's mocking me, fucking mocking me. My heart thumps hard against my chest, my palms clench to punish her and her attitude.

"Get your ass up on the bed." I snap, glaring at her with raging eyes.

Angel takes her sweet ass time doing as she's been told. Dropping her towel then sauntering over to the bed, like she has all the time in the mother fucking world. She flicks her hair seductively over her shoulder and then strains her head to view me. "Like this?" she says as she wiggles that ass playfully in the air while on all fours. Sweet Jesus.

My cock jerks at the sight.

I decide the little brat needs punishment first and foremost. Without giving her a sign of what's coming, I draw my hand into the air and smack her ass hard. "Oh, shit Finn!" her body struggles to stay upright with the shock at my palm hitting her ass. She rights herself quickly and tightens her fists into the bedsheets.

"Are you sorry?" I ask her.

Her eyes meet mine over her shoulder, her mouth parted in shock. "For what?"

Is she fucking serious? For leaving me, for not being there, not giving me what we always should have had and for the mother fucking sex toys.

I raise my hand and smack her ass again, my palm print showing on her cheek.

Angel grunts, "Yes." She swallows audibly. "I'm sorry." Her voice turns solemn.

I trail my finger down her spine, causing goosebumps to break out over her body. "Good girl." I coo gently at her, causing her spine to arch into my touch, my words.

I let my towel fall and drop my gaze toward the pile of fucking toys, making my decision. "Pass me the condoms." Angel's eyes meet mine once again in question. Wondering why I've now decided to start using condoms. Well, she's about to find out. I smirk.

The hesitation only takes a moment before she passes me the box. I open it slowly, taking my sweet ass time. I can be a cocky fucker too, darlin'. She fidgets impatiently.

I roll the condom down my thick cock, already hating the

feeling of it. Knowing what my girl feels like and knowing how she was made for me, fucking raw and bare to me, not concealed with this shit. I work my jaw from side to side.

I grab what I need and switch a vibrator on, the humming noise filling the room. Yeah, I'm not starting it on slow. None of this is going to be steady. She's going to learn who owns her the hard way, not soft, that's for sure.

I push her back down slightly so her pussy is against the vibrator. Her breathy little moans escape her naughty mouth as she drops her legs open wider. "That's right, open that pussy up for me." I squeeze a shit ton of lube on her ass cheeks and start massaging it in with my free hand, taking care around the redness of my palm print. "Angel, take the toy from me, darlin'. Play with your clit with it, understand me, just your clit."

She nods, "Just my clit."

"Good girl. Good girl darlin'." I use both my hands to rub her ass cheeks, loving the wet, greasy texture the lube leaves on her skin. My cock twitches in response, pre-cum dripping into the condom.

"Oh. Oh, Finn."

"Keep playing darlin'." I drizzle the surrounding lube around her bare asshole, fucking gorgeous. I clench my teeth as I bring the tip of my cock toward it. This is going to feel so damn good.

"Oh, my god. Yes!" She pushes her ass back onto my cock. I don't even have to fucking encourage her before she's almost fully accepted me. My teeth grind against one another, the sensation almost making me lose my load in an instant.

"Fuck darlin'."

"Yes, oh my god, Finn!" she breathes heavily. I begin to thrust my hips, hitting her ass repeatedly, my cock ramming inside her tight muscle. "Faster!" Holy fuck. My balls slap against her, the noise filling the air.

I drop my head back, gripping her hip, bruising tighter as my thrusts become more aggressive.

"Fucking take it, Angel. Take it!"

"Yes, Finn. Yes!" her breathy voice pants. I can feel the buzzing sensation of the vibrator around us.

The tingling of my balls and the rush racing through me. I quickly pull my cock out of her ass. Angel deflates and her eyes dart over her shoulder. I pull off the condom and ram into her pussy before she can question me, making her scream in ecstasy. I grab another smaller vibrator and switch it on. Angel grips the bed sheets in her fist as I push it into her ass. The rhythm matching that of my cock.

I can feel the vibrations through the wall of her muscles making my balls tighten and I cum, "Fuckkk!"

"Finnnnn. Oh god, Finn." She screeches into the mattress.

We come screaming one another's names. My body falls against hers, flattening her to the bed, my weight crushing down on her.

I suck her silky, strawberry scented neck into my mouth, marking her. Tugging with my teeth for good measure.

Now I own all of her.

All her body belongs to me.

Just the way it should have been.

Angel

Finn's breath tickles my neck as he lies on top of me. His balls now empty and his cock soft once again. His cum dripping out of me, again. I squeeze my eyes closed at the thought, wishing the potential consequences away.

Finn rolls off of me and drops down beside me. I tilt my head to meet his eyes, his handsome face now propped up on an elbow, a cocky smile gracing his lips.

I roll to face him, cupping his cheek. My fingers follow the line of his jaw, noticing the fresh scars on his face. I trace the line of the scars, wincing at the thought of him being hurt. He catches my hand in his, kissing it gently, making me smile back at him now, matching his.

Finn's eyes glance away, then they come back to mine with a look of determination. The once gentle moment now evaporated. "Is Chad Charlie's father?" he asks, his eyes completely vulnerable and uncertain. My heart pounds forcefully against my chest, my throat going dry.

Finn's eyes watch me carefully, calculating, assessing my movement. "No." I answer truthfully from under my lashes.

His shoulders relax slightly. "Who?"

I shake my head and move to get up. There's absolutely no way I'm going there, no way.

Finn grabs my wrist and pulls me back down beside him. His gaze locks onto mine, his eyes now wild. "Who?" he repeats, sterner, making me flinch at his tone.

Opening my mouth, nothing comes out. Trying again, I take a deep breath and try again. "I don't want to talk about it." Shuffling backward, I make to move, but his hand braces around my wrist, tighter this time. I squeeze my eyes shut at the intensity of his stare, the aggression behind his eyes.

"Is he in the picture?" He licks his lips nervously while scanning my face.

I shake my head.

"Has he ever?"

I shake my head, and his body relaxes once again. "Good." Just one word.

If only he knew.

Sickness waves over me, causing my whole-body to shake. I can feel the color draining from me.

"Darlin', you okay?"

I nod robotically.

His eyes drill into me with concern before they soften, and he brushes the hair from my eyes. "Just wanted to make sure I wasn't having any competition in the daddy department." He chuckles, trying to lighten the moment. He was searching for answers. That's what he was doing. And honestly? I can't blame him. He won't be getting any, though. Never.

Finn moves off the bed and begins getting dressed while peering down at me. "You fuck that Chad, dude?" He asks with a raised eyebrow.

I shake my head.

He smiles to himself. "Good girl. Gonna get you fed, darlin'. Get dressed before princess comes home, okay?"

My heart warms at his words, "home." Before my stomach plummets at the reality.

"Okay." I fake a smile, knowing this will never be our home.

"And throw the fucking toys. I'll get my own if I want them." He throws over his shoulder as he leaves the room.

My mind still stuck on his words, "home." We can never be together like that, no matter how deluded Finn is right now.

No matter how much I wish we could.

CHAPTER 9

Angel

We've been sitting on the floor playing monopoly for what feels like hours now. Ty is winning and sits smugly with a neat pile of hotels and houses littered across the board game. Charlie sits with a face like thunder, her arms folded across her chest in temper. But Finn? Finn's sincere smile fills my heart with an emotion I'm not prepared to recognize.

"Finn. Can I paint your nails?" Charlie speaks innocently out of the blue while inspecting Finn's nails with her dark eyes.

Finn chuckles uncomfortably, scratching a hand through his hair. I watch him shift on his ass, not knowing what to say to the sweet little girl staring up at him with anticipation. I stifle a smile at his reaction.

"Erm. I'm not sure nail colors are for me, princess. I guess they suit ladies more." Her eyebrows knit together in confusion before darting her eyes to Tyler. He holds his hands up proudly, wiggling his purple-colored fingers in Finn's direction, causing Finn to chuckle on an awkward laugh. I bite my lip between my teeth to stop myself from laughing. His eyes dart to mine, asking for help.

"Mom's ex-boyfriend let me," she announces, smiling sweetly at him. Yes, she's my daughter, that's for sure. She knows just what she's doing. She watches him closely for a reaction.

Finn's eyes seer into mine, causing me to blush, heat rising up my neck. "He did, huh?" his tone threatening.

"Yep," she pops the p. "But he didn't like glitter. He was..." she taps her finger to her chin then turns her head to me, searching for the word. "... Mommy said he was vanilla, it means boring. He was vanilla, right Mommy?" Finn spits his beer out on a choke, covering his white t-shirt. My eyes bug out at her innocent words.

"Vanilla, huh?" He questions, glaring at me.

Ty grins happily, enjoying me squirming under Finn's accusing eyes.

Finn clears his throat, his eyes never leaving mine. "You know what, princess? I'm feeling the glitter varnish right now. How 'bout you go get them and show me what you've got?"

"Yay!!! I love you so much Finn!" Charlie jumps up and throws herself at Finn. His eyes meet mine over her shoulder. His lip curving into a sly smile. I roll my eyes at his childish behavior. But grateful all the same.

Finn

I'm laid on the couch trying my damn best to get some sleep. Angel was clear I wasn't welcome in her bed tonight. She didn't want to confuse Charlie? Yeah, what the fuck ever. I'll give her tonight, but this is happening, and princess will be onboard with it, especially after I let her paint my damn toes too. I now have rainbow fucking nails, half my fingertips covered too, but honestly, I don't give a shit.

I punch the pillow again and pull my duvet higher. I've slept in a war zone more comfortable than this goddamn thing.

I'm just about to relax when the soft creak of a door has my senses on alert. I tilt my head toward the hallway wondering if Charlie has got up for the bathroom, but my eyes catch on the white of a t-shirt, my t-shirt. My mouth goes dry at the sight of her.

Angel's smooth legs move closer toward me and I suck in a breath, hoping I've played it cool enough for her not to realize I'm actually awake watching her.

"Finn?" her soft, low voice sends my heart racing.

I groan out loud, feigning sleep. "Finn. Could I…?" her voice is a soft whisper with a hint of trepidation.

I sit up and take her in. She's tugging the t-shirt down, her body shaking. My eyes scan her face, her lip quivers, and she seems scared half to death. I glance back at the door and wonder what the fuck has happened. My eyebrows knit in confusion. "You good?" I query, unsure what's wrong.

She nods, but I don't miss the uncertainty in her eyes. They shimmer with unshed tears as she stands watching me. "You wanna get in here?" I tilt my head toward the duvet and open it up. Before I have time to question her further, she practically leaps under the duvet with me, snuggling in, her back to my chest. Squeezing my arm around her tighter and her whole-body relaxes against me. "I wish I could keep you," she whispers so lightly I know I wasn't meant to hear her. I breathe in her strawberry scent and kiss the top of her head with a silent promise.

There's no fucking way I'm leaving.

You'd have to kill me first.

CHAPTER 10

Finn

Charlie is back to school tomorrow and then off to camp on Tuesday, so I decided we needed to do a little family bonding.

So, after Angel's little meltdown about not going out to lunch, she finally relented when I got princess onboard with the idea.

Angel walks out of her bedroom in a huff with nothing more than booty shorts and a crop top of some sort on, showing way too much fucking flesh. My temper flares and my palms twitch beside me. Has she been wearing this shit all this time? Does she not realize the attention she'll receive? Or is that what she wants? My pulse throbs in my forehead at her blasé attitude.

Her eyebrows furrow in confusion at my expression. "What's wrong?"

I breathe deeply to rein in my anger. My words come out seething, "What's wrong is, you need to go back to your room and cover-up. Jesus, you don't walk the streets dressed like that Angel! Christ." I brush a hand through my hair, sucking in the air.

Angel's nostrils flare and she crosses her arms over her chest, pushing those glorious tits up even higher. My tongue darts out to wet my dry lips. "I can wear whatever I fucking want!" she lifts her chin higher. Brat.

I take a step closer, which causes her to step back. "You want me to spank your bratty ass? That it? Angel being a naughty girl?" I quiz with a lift of my eyebrow, "Go change, or I'll make you." I shrug a shoulder of indifference. Her cheeks pinked with either embarrassment or desire, flushing, appearing all the way down to those…

"Fine, I'll go change, but only because I want to." She huffs like a petulant child and spins on her heel. I grin smugly, pleased with myself and my girl for listening to her man.

"Finn?" Charlie's sweet voice breaks through my thoughts. "Do I look okay? Or do I gotta change too?" Charlie holds her arms out for approval. I scan my princess, cute as fuck. Little blue legging things and a rainbow-colored unicorn t-shirt with some high-top sneakers. My princess looks adorable.

My voice is soft for my little girl. "You look perfect, princess."

Charlie's lip curls into a smile. "I do?" I nod at her.

Charlie sighs, "George Adams said I always look like my Mama has no money."

My chest flares, my teeth ache, I step toward Charlie. "Yeah? George Adams is a coc…"

"Whoa there, big guy." Ty's palm rests on my chest as he laughs mockingly. "Calm your tits," he whispers in my ear. "Little George is a seven-year-old spoiled brat." His eyebrows raise in some sort of amusement.

"I want his address." I spit out with all seriousness.

Ty steps back and assesses me. His eyes bulge. "Oh shit. You're serious, aren't you?"

I nod. "Jesus, Finn. He's a kid. Kids are..." Tyler's hands float around the room. "Kids."

"Don't give a shit; this little prick upsets my girls; little fucker's parents can pay."

"Are we ready? What are you guys whispering about?" Angel moves from foot to foot as my eyes scan down her delicious body. God damn, my girl is stunning. Her ass fills her jeans and her top is now covering her stomach. Her cherry red hair flows in waves down her back, and she pulls on a leather jacket to finish the look as she glances over her shoulder at Ty and me.

"Huh?" I ask, completely fucking confused as to what she just asked.

"Ready?" her smile spreads across her face. I march toward my girl, swooping down and tugging her lips between my teeth. I hear her breath still. I grip ahold of her hands and pull them above her head, pushing my waist into her stomach, letting her feel what she does to me, my hardness strokes against her.

"Erm. Hello? Seven-year-old and suppressed gay guy here!" Ty chimes from behind while clearing his throat.

I take a step back and stare at my girl. Gently, I tuck a wave of her cherry locks behind her pierced ears. "Fucking hot, darlin'. Gonna spank that ass tonight." Angel's lips part in response.

"When I'm an adult, I'm going to get myself a boyfriend who kisses me just like that." Charlie points at me.

"No!" I spin around to face princess, "Not a chance, sweetheart." Her nose scrunches up. "You don't get a boyfriend until I say so." I smile back at her. The kid goes from confused to all-out delight. A smile graces her little face; she nods at me.

"Come on, let's go." Angel tugs me along and out the door with Charlie hot on our heels.

Angel

We walked the entire length of the park with Finn darting after a squealing Charlie. My daughter is absolutely besotted with him. My heart tugs at my chest, followed by a pool of dread in my stomach. I want to keep him, keep this, the three of us. But it's not even in the realm of possibility. I'm just not sure how I'm going to end it. Maybe I should have let Finn think I cheated? That way, he might hate me and leave us alone? A wave of sickness runs through me. I could never hurt him like that. Never. It was bad enough when he actually thought I was capable of something like that.

My heart hammers in my chest as I watch Finn swoop down and pick up Charlie. Her blonde locks fall around her face like a curtain closing. If he knew the truth, would he feel the same about her? About me? My footsteps falter at the panic coursing through me; my throat clogs up. No. No, he can never find out. That's not even an option. Never.

"Hey, you ready for some lunch?" Finn asks as he easily tugs Charlie onto his shoulders. Her small hands clutch the leather of his jacket. I nod. "You okay? You've gone quiet suddenly." Finn's eyes roam over my body as if searching for a problem. If only he knew the issue was inside and not visible to the naked eye. Most of them, anyway.

I shake my head as if shaking away the thoughts. "Fine, just got lost there for a minute."

Finn's eyes darken, and his jaw tics in frustration. He ducks his head slightly to speak in my ear, his voice deep and menacing, "and I told you, you'll never be lost from me again. Got it?" He takes a step back, far enough for me to stare directly into his eyes. I swallow thickly, unable to find my words. I nod at him like an adoring puppy. His shoulders visibly relax and his lips transform into a genuine smile. What the fuck? He's certifiable, I swear.

Finn takes hold of my hand and grips it in his tightly as though I'm going to run away from him.

———

Walking into the diner for lunch, Finn's hand finds the lower part of my back. I unknowingly relax into him with ease, the familiarity setting in.

"Can I get you guys a table?" The hostess asks Finn. Not even giving me a second glance. What a bitch. I scan her; her blonde hair falls over her shoulders and down to her ass. Her tits look fake, but yeah, even I can admit how good they look. I hate her. Instantly fucking hate her. I catch a glimpse of my own reflection in the window beside me. No longer the innocent-looking blonde I once was. Is that what Finn prefers? Jealousy curses around inside me, but also self-loathing. Why couldn't everything just be how it was? Why did everything have to change?

Finn's eyes sharpen on the bitch. "Yeah, a booth at the back." He points over my shoulder.

"Sure," the tramp smiles back at him. Annoyance grows inside me, and I bite my cheek to rein in my thoughts.

We walk through the diner toward the back. Finn's hand never leaves my back, guiding me. The hostess motions for us to take the seats and she hands out the menus, lingering over the top of Finn. Charlie sits next to the window; I squeeze in next to her, and Finn sits opposite me. Charlie's eyes light up when she sees the desserts. "Can we have dessert too, Mommy?"

I nod while watching the interaction between Finn and the hostess.

"Can I get you anything else?" The tramp pushes her tits up higher and smiles adoringly at my man.

Finn snarls. "Yeah. If you're the server, get me a new one. I don't want one that eye fucks me in front of my family."

The tramp's mouth gapes open, then closes. I want to do a little victory dance, shout from the rooftops. But I bite my lip and try not to laugh as she scurries away like a little rat.

Finn

Charlie munches happily on her burger. She's already on her second strawberry milkshake and getting ready for another. I watch my princess in awe at how much like her mother she is. Apart from her eyes, the dark eyes both draw me in and make me shudder.

I flick my eyes back over to the table to my left, annoyed with the blonde prick that's now watching my Angel eat her fries. Granted, my girl sure knows how to eat seductively, but who the fuck does this prick think he is? His eyes fixate on my Angel's chest and it takes every bit of willpower to keep my ass in my seat. I fight the need to rip his eyes out and not make a scene in front of my girls. I scrub a hand through my hair and take a toothpick out of my pocket. Desperate to take the edge off my rage.

"So, Cal now has a son and daughter? Wow, I bet he's an amazing father." My eyes flit back to Angel. I'd given her a brief update on our growing family back home while walking around the park; she was so thrilled when I told her Con and Will were not only together but have a child, one that Con didn't find out about until only recently.

"And Cal's son Reece? How old is he?"

"Sixteen. But he's a genius, better than Oscar." I add with a smile. I watch my darlin's eyes bug out. Everyone knows how intelligent yet quirky my older brother Oscar is. "Reece has high functioning autism. The kid masterminded bringing his parents back together." I explain.

"Wow. That's incredible, so you're an uncle." Angel grins at me.

"I'm a dad darlin'." I nod toward Charlie, who is happily coloring and then smile back at Angel. Her color has drained from her face and her expression is now coated in doubt. Yeah, fuck that. I lean over the table and get in her face. "Mean. Every. Fucking. Word." I punctuate them before I slowly move back into my seat. Angel's throat bobs and she slowly swallows, darting her eyes away from mine.

"Yeah, that's what worries me." I hear her words softly spoken, but I hear them all the same. Whatever she thinks is going to happen between us isn't. I'll show her. She doesn't have a choice, not this time.

"So, tell me about how you met Tyler and Chad; what's the deal with them?"

Angel watches me closely, thinking her words through before actually saying them. "We met when I was pregnant with Charlie." She dips a fry in her ketchup slowly, deep in thought. "I was looking for work, approached the club. Chad took pity on me and Tyler worked at the bar. We've been friends ever since." She shrugs as if it's nothing. But I've witnessed the bond between her and Tyler. Charlie even calls him Uncle. They're her family. I can see it in not only their eyes but their actions, too.

My eyes once again catch onto the blonde douche. That not only is eye fucking my girl like a piece of meat, but is now encouraging his friends to ogle her. My jaw tics in annoyance, my hands clench into fists.

"Finn, Finn. Finn, are you listening to me?" Charlie nudges me with her hand.

I glance at Charlie. "Sorry, sweetheart. You good?"

"Yes, thank you. But can you color with me?"

I smile back at my princess, so well-mannered and polite; her mama has done amazing with her. A sudden pain in my heart makes my stomach plummet at the thought of Angel being a mother without me there. I should have been there for her. Me, not any fucker else. I try to swallow the anger and guilt and concentrate on the cute little blonde girl sitting next to her mom. "I've got the princess. You do the trees." Charlie nods at me with a smile and starts humming while coloring in the lines. Smart too.

———

Movement catches my attention from the corner of my eye. The blonde prick rises and moves toward the restrooms. Game fucking on, motherfucker.

I jump out of my seat. "Finn, where are you going?" Angel startles.

"Need to piss darlin', back in a minute." Her eyes bulge at my crass words.

I swing open the restroom door and assess the little prick who dared to eye fuck my girl in front of me. Time to be taught a lesson, mother fucker.

His eyes catch mine in the mirror above his head as he continues to piss into the urinal, oblivious to the pain that's going to hit him.

I take a slow, calculated step toward him; his shoulders straighten as if only just realizing I'm a threat and about to rain down hell on him. I curl my lip smugly in response.

"Why the hell are you staring at me like that?" he splutters.

I take another step forward. "Why the hell you staring at my girl the way you were?" My eyes never leave his. His Adam's apple bobs nervously.

He feigns confidence, shrugging. "She has a nice rack, just appreciating it."

Oh, no, he fucking didn't. My spine goes ramrod straight as my legs move before I can tell them to slow down. I grab ahold of the fucker's neck and smash his face into the mirror.

"Ow. Oh, please." He stumbles over his words as I strike his face against the mirror again. "P... please."

His dick flops about. "Hold your dick out!" I demand. The guy's eyes bulge out through the blood trailing down his panic-ridden face. "Hold. It. Out!" I grit out.

"Please, don't."

I move toward him, and he backs up against the wall.

Quickly, his hands grip his dick. I sneer down at the offending, flaccid little fucker. "I'm s... sorry."

I pull out my knife and flick it open, not giving the guy a second glance; his hands shake as I move toward him, gripping my knife punishingly. I surge my knife into his dick like a skewer before withdrawing it with a swift shake of my hand.

An ear-piercing scream comes from the fuck wit's mouth. "Jesus, please." I step back and assess my handiwork. Not bad. I grin at the dude menacingly before turning on my heel. I painstakingly wash my hands, not taking my eyes off the dude who is leaning against the piss-tiled wall, shuddering. His eyes don't meet mine, but he's watching me. Chicken shit can't even be a man. I straighten my leather jacket and push a wet hand through my unruly hair, styling it in the mirror while the dude all but pisses himself in terror. A laugh catches in my throat, knowing he won't be pissing right for a while.

"Jesus, you're insane!" he screams out.

I chuckle, "Yeah, I know." I give him a wink and leave the restroom with a spring in my step and feeling mildly better.

CHAPTER 11

Finn

    I wake to arguing, darting up on the couch as my eyes shoot around the room, searching for a target. Paranoia and insomnia have become a part of me since leaving the Army. I struggle to wind down and switch off. I'm always hyper-aware of my surroundings, so the fact I slept so soundly with Angel tucked under my blanket once again is still a little shocking. Being awoken to unexpected sounds in an unfamiliar place automatically puts all my training to use, but at the same time, triggers my emotions.

I relax as soon as I realize the voices are coming from Tyler and Angel. They're facing off in the kitchen, Tyler's hands flying in the air on every other word. "I'm just saying Finn is here. You'll be perfectly fine," he whispers.

A spoon clinks beside me, and my eyes move across to the little girl sitting cross-legged on the floor, watching me with curiosity. Her mouth was half full of cornflakes. "They're talking about you." She points toward the kitchen with the spoon and a toothy smile on her face, the milk dripping down her chin.

I duck my head back down to the pillow, out of sight. I

watch my little ally closely. "What are they saying?" Keeping my voice low.

Charlie grins at me, cornflakes leaving the sides of her mouth, making my lip curl up in a humorous grin. "Tyler wants to go away on vacation with his boy toy, but Mommy doesn't want him to leave," she sighs. I widen my eyes at Charlie's words; clearly, my princess is used to eavesdropping. Fucking boy toy, I'll spank Angel's ass for that one.

"Why doesn't she want him to leave?" My eyebrows furrow, my voice soft.

Charlie munches her cereal then rolls her eyes dramatically, "Whenever Tyler leaves, we go stay with Uncle Chad," she pauses before starting again, dragging her word out, "Pluusss, I go to camp tomorrow, and she doesn't want to be on her own."

Before I get the chance to ask anymore, Charlie jumps up, leaving me behind, and walks into the kitchen area.

"So, Finn, now you're awake, care to have an opinion on the matter?" Tyler smiles at me pointedly while walking over and dropping into the chair beside the couch.

"Ty!" Angel warns, her jaw tightening.

He wafts his hand in her direction as if to shush her. "I was just telling Chels I'm going to Florida with Troy this afternoon. Chels likes company while I'm gone, isn't that right, Chels?" He raises an eyebrow in her direction. I glance at Angel, her jaw sharp and jutting out at Tyler's words. "Anyway, I suggested she go stay with Chad."

My spine straightens at his name. "Like fucking hell she will. I'm staying here," my demanding tone, giving no room for negotiation. Tyler grins cunningly at me, little prick.

Angel sighs, defeated. But I smile wider, tucking my folded arms under my head, loving how a plan comes together.

———

Angel and Tyler spend the day panic buying last-minute items for Charlie's school trip.

When Charlie gets home from school, she's in full excitement mode, helping Angel pack her camping gear. It reminds me of when me and my brothers would go camping with my uncle. The entire summer we would countdown for him to take us away from the expectations of our father. Apart from Oscar, who had a thing about being outdoors and around bugs, dirt and other shit that triggered his anxieties, it was the highlight of the year for us kids. I smile to myself at the memories. Princess is going to have an amazing time, that's for sure.

"Hey Finn, listen. I need you to promise me something while I'm away." I turn from making a coffee to face Tyler. My eyes make a quick assessment of him. Worry lines his face, and he stands a little uncomfortable against the countertop.

"Sure," I nod for him to elaborate.

"I need you to not push Chels," he fidgets with his hands and ducks his head away from my gaze.

My spine straightens automatically on the use of her fake name, irritation marring my skin. Tyler recognizes the change in me, his voice low. "She's just delicate, you know." I give him a nod in recognition, "Just… just don't push her, okay? I don't want you to push her away." He glances over his shoulder, leaving the words playing out in my mind, "Don't push her away." Does he know something I don't? He watches me closely, almost as if waiting for me to catch up with what he's saying. My heart hammers against my chest violently.

I lick my lips and go in for the kill, "She planning on going away?" My palms sweat with anxiousness.

Tyler's eyes stare into my own guiltily, "I… I think she's scared."

A rush of panic consumes me, and I grip the counter to steady myself. She wants to fucking leave me, Jesus. I scrub a hand through my hair. I can't go through that again. Won't.

I choke on my words. "I won't let her leave me. Not again." I shake my head, refusing to acknowledge the thought, determination pouring from each one of my words.

"She doesn't want to leave you, Finn, but she doesn't think she has a choice." Tyler watches my reactions closely. The fucking riddles these pair are talking in are driving my mind insane; I just need someone to explain to me what the fuck is happening.

My eyes meet Tyler's and I swallow thickly. "You know why she left me?" I ask him vulnerably.

His shoulders sag and his eyes glaze over with pity. "She didn't have a choice."

Anger fills my veins. Of course, she had a fucking choice. There's always a choice. "She tell you I joined the forces to get us away from our families? Away from our lives, did she tell you I wanted to marry her? She tell you that, huh?" I ask him, anger rising in my voice.

He nods solemnly, swallowing hard on emotion. "Yeah, she did."

"Did she tell you she left while I was on tour in Iraq? I called home, and she wasn't fucking there? Gone, not even a fucking note." Rage boils my blood, my words laced in hate, "She tell you I lost my little fucking brother? And she wasn't there? Packed the fuck up and went to the West Coast living the fucking high life without me!" I stab my finger to my chest, hurt taking over the hate-filled words, "She tell you that, Ty?"

"She did. She told me everything, Finn." His voice is gentle, soothing, almost trying to reassure me, sympathetic, and supportive all in one.

I take him in, a silence between us. Emotion makes me stumble over my words, "She... she tell you why? Why she left me?" My eyes glaze over and I will away the feelings surfacing again.

"She did." His eyes drill into mine as if trying to silently communicate something to me. "She didn't have a choice." He gives me a firm, solid nod, as if expecting me to accept his word. My body lags at his words. She didn't have a choice.

"You gonna tell me why?" Desperation seeps from me. I stare into his eyes, hoping for answers.

He shakes his head gently. "I'm sorry," his eyes move away guiltily, "I can't betray her trust, Finn. But she didn't want to leave you." He turns on his heel, and I watch as he walks away.

So many unanswered questions on my mind, consumed with the sheer panic at the thoughts of losing her again. Her and Charlie.

My head pounds with the tension, my shoulders ache with tightness, anxiety rippling through me. I won't let her leave me. Not again. Not ever.

———

After Tyler left to go on vacation with his boy toy me; Angel and Charlie ordered in pizza. We watched some chick flick thing about a group of kids who enter singing contests while at a camp. Charlie loved every minute of it. I glance over at her small frame, curled up on the chair, a blanket tucked around her little body and her familiar blonde locks dragging down to the floor. A floppy pink rabbit teddy shoved under her arm. She's the spitting image of her mama at that age, a little fucking Angel. A primal surge of love engulfs me at the sight of her.

I still remember the first time I saw Angel, innocent green eyes peeking up from under her lashes, as she clutched her bible to her chest. Little Annabel Mathers took my breath away, and I was ten years fucking old. I knew she was mine; I'd never want another girl for the rest of my life. She imprinted on me, left a scar on my heart that only she could heal. Her mama was a selfish bitch who treated Angel like shit, even forgetting to feed her. She was a whore to the so-called good men of the church community.

A cruel junkie who didn't care where and what her little girl was doing. I wanted to rescue my little Angel and keep her safe. My ma saw it too. She welcomed her into our home through the church groups, teaching her how to cook and sew. Whenever I walked into our kitchen and saw her there, our eyes would meet, and she'd blush, a cute pink splaying over her cheeks. She didn't even spare my brothers a second glance; it was just her and me. We were meant to be, even back then, sneaking little kisses in the garden, holding her hand, and then dropping it as soon as I heard my brothers or parents. I was determined nobody would take her away from me, so I didn't want to give them cause to.

We were a secret until High School, then every boy that glanced in her direction got a fist to his filthy mouth or a smashed nose so they couldn't breathe in her strawberry scent. We had all our firsts together, and I couldn't give a shit if she would have been my last. Everything I had belonged to her. There would be no one else. Never.

My stomach roils at the thought that Angel created my little princess with someone else. I shut my eyes and try to rein off the turmoil in my head.

Staring down at Charlie, I gently push Angel from my side. I tilt my head in Charlie's direction. "I'm going to put her to bed."

I lower myself in front of Charlie and scoop her up, blanket and all. Her eyes flutter open slightly, "Finn?"

"Shhh, it's okay princess; I'm just going to tuck you into bed." I make my way down the hallway and into her room. Pink every fucking where. A single bed pushed against the wall with a net canopy, and sparkly lights guide me toward the bed. I gently lower her down and tuck her into her pink duvet. She wriggles into the bedding, and I watch her closely, not wanting to leave her just yet. "Finn?" Her voice soft.

"Yeah, princess?"

"Are you going to leave when I'm at camp? Will you come back?" My heart skips a beat at her words.

I crouch down beside her and smooth out her messy blonde locks, her smattering of freckles highlighted by the lights, just like her mama's. "No, sweetness," her body sags before I can even explain. I chuckle to myself. "I'm going to persuade your Mama to move, so you can both live with me. Would you like that?"

Her eyes light up. "Do I get my own room?"

I grin at her naivety. "Yeah, princess. A big room, where we can get you an enormous bed." I gaze around the room and spread my arm out. "Pink with all this cute stuff if you want? Anything you want, sweetness." My eyes meet hers, and I hope she can see the truth behind my words because I will give her anything she wants, her and her mama.

She smiles happily into the duvet. "Mommy said that you went away to be a soldier and fight to get a better life. Did you do it?"

My smile tightens at her innocent words, part happy that Angel discussed me and yet part mad at the reminder. I scrub a hand through my hair as she watches me expectedly, "I did. Did she tell you anything else?"

"She said you were the hottest guy she'd ever seen." She snickers at her words.

I grin at her words. "Yeah. She was right about that. Anything else?"

"She said she wishes she could keep you forever." My heart soars. My girl wants me as much as I want her. I fucking knew it.

"She can keep me; you can too. We belong together, me, your Mommy and you. You're our little princess; you get that?"

She nods, with the cutest grin spreading across her face.

I bend down and kiss her forehead. "You get some sleep

now princess. You've got an amazing trip to look forward to tomorrow."

"Okay, Finn-Fitty." She giggles, making my heart pump with fucking joy.

I close the door with a soft click.

CHAPTER 12

Angel

I wait patiently on my bed for Finn to leave Charlie's room. It feels like he's been in there forever. I can hear the low murmurs and the soft giggles of my little girl. My heart fills with love at the thought of their interaction.

I can hear Finn walking around the apartment, expecting to find me on the couch. Before making his way over to my room.

Kneeling on the bed with my legs wide open. My cherry red locks wild over one shoulder. I'm wearing bright red matching suspenders and panties that barely cover my pussy. My bra pushes my already heavy breasts higher, my nipples on full display.

Finn opens the door; his eyes find mine in an instant. Shock graces his handsome face before it's quickly replaced with an unyielding need of desire. His eyes trace over my body and he sucks in a shallow breath, his chest rising rapidly. He closes the door and saunters toward the bed.

I crawl on all fours and meet him at the end. He surveys my body, his eyes trailing over my back to my ass and then back to my face. His cocky grin is firmly in place, his hand gently trails over my cheek and jawline. "Fucking hot, darlin'. So fucking hot," he pants breathlessly, his mouth open a little in awe.

I move my hands toward his belt and begin fumbling to open it. He watches my movement intently. His hands clenching and unclenching into fists, holding himself back, letting me take charge. I smirk at the thought.

I tug down his jeans. His cock is jutting out of his boxers, the end sticky in anticipation. I quickly roll down his underwear as my tongue darts out and licks my lower lip. Finn grips my hair tightly with one hand as I watch his thick, hard cock jerk in response to my touch.

I explore him with my hand and eyes. Taking in every detail the old and new. The vein protrudes along his hardness, his balls heavy and soft, free of hair. The tip of his cock looks desperate and angry, red and throbbing. I swipe my thumb over the top and smear his thick pre-come around the head. Finn jerks and sucks in a breath, his hold tightening.

I glance up into his eyes. They're hooded. His pupils blown, his mouth slightly parted.

"Darlin'," he warns.

I hang my mouth open wide and lower my lips. I watch him seductively as he chews his lip in annoyance and desperation. My mouth opens, taunting his shaft.

His hand pushes my head closer; his hips thrust out in my direction, eager to enter my throat. I swipe my tongue over the head of his cock and stroke my hand over his balls. "Fuck darlin', like that." He thrusts hard, pushing himself into my mouth, not giving me a choice in the matter. Wetness pools between my legs and I fidget to stroke the material of my panties against my clit. Finn chuckles knowingly at my movement.

I work my tongue up and down his cock, kissing the velvety hardness and gently sucking his skin before lowering my mouth onto him. I suck with desperation to please him, the salty taste encompassing my mouth spurring me on. Finn thrusts his hips erratically and tightens his hand in my hair, the sting of his hold unexpectedly turning me on.

"Fuck, like that. God, damn, you look so fucking hot sucking my cock, darlin'. So fucking hot!" he thrusts hard, causing me to gag. "Fuck, take it, take it." His hand pulls harshly on my hair, guiding my mouth up and down on his cock, completely fucking my face. He chants, making me moan around his length, "Holy fuck darlin'." His mouth parts in awe as he rears back and rams his cock into my mouth once more, his cum flooding my mouth. "Fuckkk!" He loses his footing slightly before stifling a laugh.

He leaves my mouth with a pop, stroking my face affectionately, then gently brushing his fingers over my lips. His thumb pushes a bit of cum into my mouth and I open for him in an instant. My tongue swirls around his thumb, his eyes watching the movement.

Finn pulls away and drags his t-shirt over his head, dropping it to the floor. His dog tags drop against his golden chest. His chiseled abs on display make me shift against my panties. I follow the small scattering of hairs down toward his cock, still heavy. How the hell can he still be hard? I swallow at the thought of his stamina. He kicks his jeans and boxers aside, and I watch over my shoulder as he clambers onto the top of the bed, his head resting up on the pillows.

"Drop the bra, darlin', let me see those tits bounce." I do as I'm told. Slowly, I drop the straps of my bra, my tits almost spilling out. I lick my lips at Finn and then drop the bra to the bed. "Get your ass up here and let my tongue lick that pussy out. You wet?" Desire utterly consumes me with his filthy mouth, and at the thought of his tongue licking me, I nod. Shifting off the bed, I walk around to the top and stand in front of Finn, gazing down into his gorgeous blue eyes, the heat from them warming me, making me squeeze my legs in anticipation. Finn's arms stretch out toward me, and he rips the panties from my hips, the sharpness of his action making them cut into my sides. He lets them fall freely to the floor. "God damn beautiful," his eyes scan up and down my body, landing on my tits. He smacks my thigh hard. "Up!" His tongue trails out over his lips.

I climb over Finn's body and up toward his waiting mouth, perching my legs on either side of his head. His eyes stare up at me with admiration. My heart pounds at his gaze, trapped in a moment between us, the air stilling around us. His eyes flick back down to my tits, and his hands move up to massage them softly at first. He swallows harshly and then kneads them harder, his thumbs grazing my nipples. "Darlin', get that clit in my mouth, real fucking quick, while I play with these babies."

I groan at his words and hover my pussy over his mouth. A hand leaves my breast and grips my ass cheek, pulling me into his waiting mouth. I glance down at his eyes, and they close slightly when his tongue laps through my folds as if embracing the taste, his hand joining the other once again, punishing my breasts with the squeezing, tugging and tweaking of my nipples. The feeling is sensational. I grip onto the headboard in front of me, riding his face. The slurping sounds of him lapping away my juices fill the room. Fuck, that's hot.

I move on his mouth, back and forth, over and over. Spreading my legs further, he moans in approval; the vibration hitting my clit. "Oh god, Finn." I throw my head back as I ride his face shamelessly, my hair falling down my spine, swaying with the motion.

His tongue turns and swirls around my clit and through my folds, the wetness and noises turning me on further.

The buildup of my orgasm is easy to reach. He eats me out like a madman. A man devoted to the taste of my pussy. The thought makes me push down on his tongue, the scruff of his jaw hitting between my thighs, creating a delicious overload of sensations. My hands turn white, gripping the headboard, and I let loose, fucking his face fiercely. "Fuck, Finn. Oh, fuck!" I can feel the vibrations of his mouth, the moans smothered by my own ecstasy as I unleash wantonly on his face.

The graze of his stubble around my ass cheeks and the pinch of my pierced nipple sends me over the edge. I screech and cry out, "Fiiinnn, oh shit!"

My movements stutter as I come down from my high. Finn throws me onto my back and quickly situates himself between my legs. He pulls my legs up over his shoulders and rams his cock into me with such force the bed slams against the wall.

His face contorted with a possessive stare, sending a thrill up my spine. I grip my breasts and push them together, loving the feeling of his hard cock slamming into me over and over. The veins on his neck and forehead are protruding, spurring me on. "Finn, harder. Harder!"

"Oh, fuck darlin'. Fuck!" He slams again, then leans forward. My legs drop and encompass his waist tightly. He grips my throat with force, and I lick my lips appreciatively. His nostrils flare, and he rams into me. The tightening of his fingers sends a shock wave of desire through my veins. I come hard. My spine straightens, my legs tense, and my pussy clenches desperately around his solid cock, squeezing his own orgasm from him. I relish in the feeling of his cock expanding and his cum hitting my inner walls, coating them with his essence. He bites into my tit and grunts at his release, sucking my skin into his mouth as if masking his own words. The sharpness of his teeth drags out my orgasm.

Finn sags onto my body, his cum seeping from my pussy as his cock, finally spent, weakens. I stroke his hair and keep my legs wrapped tightly around him. Loving the feeling of this gorgeous man between my legs and on my chest. My heart soars, refusing to accept the inevitable.

He gently kisses over my heart before moving his lips up to mine. Our eyes meet. So much unsaid between us but the need for one another taking over. My lips meet his in a soft, delicate kiss. The touch of his lips and his scent make me grip his hair tightly to hold him in place, keep him in place, to never let him go. I can already feel his cock hardening between us. His tongue searches my mouth almost desperately, hungrily tangling with my own. My heart beats so much between us it hurts. I close my eyes at the throbbing pain in my heart.

Finn moves slowly between us, gently rocking inside me. His elbows on either side of my head, he stares down at me as his body becomes alive once again.

He swallows harshly. The look of pure admiration and love in his eyes is too much to bear. He's making love to me. I try to push him away. "Finn, stop!" My chest pounds against him, desperate to stop these feelings between us, knowing how it's got to end. "What are you doing? Stop." I screech out on a choked breath, pushing roughly against his chest.

He grips my wrists and holds them at the side of my head, forcing me to let him be. "I'm making love to you, darlin'," he smiles at me and braces his legs on the bed, his full weight on me, determined not to let me move away.

I shake my head, tears escaping my eyes. Not wanting to accept his feelings. We never said the words. Never.

"Look at me!" he barks while still moving. "Fucking look at me, Angel." His voice is softer this time, almost begging.

I refuse and turn my head. He grips my chin in one hand, forcing my head to face him while his other holds my wrists above my head. My vision is blurry. I stare straight into his blue eyes, pure devotion staring right back at me. "I fucking love you. You hear? Fuck. I love you." I choke at his words. My lip quivers.

He moves faster now, pounding into me, "say it!" He snaps. "Fucking say it, Angel!" The bed hits the wall, again and again, his grip on my chin loosens and he moves his fingers to my clit, pressing it harshly; he lowers his head into my face until I can only see his eyes. "Fucking. Say. It!" He punctuates the words with each thrust.

I swallow hard, not wanting to admit my true feelings. "I love you," I gasp them out, low, barely audible, but he hears them. His mouth drops open, and he comes with a shudder; pressing harder and pinching my clit I soon join him.

His head drops into the crook of my neck and I cradle him to me with tears streaming down my face.

CHAPTER 13

F **inn**

I tuck her under my arm and stroke her hair, the red shimmering among the moonlight from the curtains. "You gonna let me stay in your bed tonight?"

Angel shakes her head gently against my chest.

"You know I'm not going anywhere, right? You know I'm here to stay?" I question her.

She fiddles with my dog tags between her fingers. "I know. Just not tonight. Not with Charlie..." She leaves her words unsaid. I know she thinks Charlie might not understand, but me and princess are both on board with our plans, and I smile smugly at her naivety, agreeing to leave her bedroom for tonight, knowing it will be the last time.

"Tell me more about your family, Finn," her voice gentle and vulnerable.

"You mean your family? Right? They're your family too, Angel, you know that." She freezes in my arms, but I ignore her unease and continue. "So I told you Con has a little boy now."

She smiles into my chest, and I continue on, "yeah, him and Will, they finally made it. Shit Angel, you missed so fucking much." My throat bobs and my heart races. "I… I needed you, darlin'."

Angel's chin wobbles. "I'm so sorry." My fingers stroke her hair and I nod, knowing if I want to keep her, I need to approach the pending conversation gently. I'm just not very fucking patient. I brush a hand through my hair and sigh.

"Bren's still a miserable bastard, he's just like Da." I shake my head at the thought of my older brother. He'll never have a woman by his side. He's too damn pigheaded and abrupt for a start. Angel giggles, so much like Charlie it's uncanny. "Cal, fuck darlin', his life is insane. He has Reece, his teenage son, and a baby girl."

I decided to tell her a bit more about Cal and his family. "You remember him bleating on about a girl in Vegas?"

Angel thinks for a moment, then bites her lip with a smile. "Well, that was a woman named Lily. Long story fucking short, Reece is like a genius hacker or some shit. Tracked Cal down by stealing millions from us; anyway they're happily married with a little girl, Chloe. Cal is a fucking mother hen, proper stress head darlin'." Angel grins at my assertion. It couldn't be any more truthful. Since Cal discovered Lily and Reece, the guy has seriously lost his balls.

"Ma and Da are still going strong. Da handed over the business for Bren to lead after Keenan died. Ma was in pieces for so long. The grandbabies have helped."

Angel watches me closely. "Did they find who hurt Keenan?"

I scrub a hand through my hair. Uncomfortable with the direction of the conversation, I struggle with anything Keenan related. "Kinda. We knew it was from a Russian gang. We made an example of a few."

Angel winces at my words, and I elaborate. "Oscar thinks there's more to it. Swear to Christ; the dude suffers from paranoia among all the other shit. He can't just be fucking happy we dealt with it." I bite the words out, annoyed with my brother.

Angel sits up quickly, her cherry locks fall over her tits, "why does he think that?" She rubs her hands together with a look of nervousness.

I stroke my hands up her arm, and she jerks slightly, making me scan her face in confusion. She's sat watching me, waiting for an answer. I shrug. "You know what he's like. Just a conspiracy theory of his, nothing to worry about. Swear darlin'." I stare into her eyes to reassure her, and she nods before tugging the sheets off and striding into the bathroom.

"You want me to take the couch now, darlin'?" I speak loudly toward the closed bathroom door, hearing her piss.

"Please."

I scrub a hand through my hair. Yeah, What. The. Fuck. Ever. Last god damn night, that's for fucking sure.

———

A gut-wrenching scream makes me shoot up and propel myself forward. Stumbling over the sheets on the couch, I slam into the wall in my haste. Wishing I'd pulled my fucking Glock out of my bag, I push the door to Angel's room open so hard it hits the wall.

I scan the room quickly with my eyes, Angel's alone but clearly in distress. My body relaxes slightly, knowing she's safe.

She bellows and grips the sheets, the awful sound stilling my body, freezing my veins. She's clearly having a nightmare. I move toward her, taking in her distress. Her eyes are wide open, but not seeing a goddamn thing.

Her palms fist the sheets as she screeches on all fours, her mouth open wide in terror, desperately gasping for air. "Please..." she begs, facing the wall. "Please don't..." I swallow thickly at her words, my body trembling as I watch her trauma unfold. "I won't tell. I swear I won't tell," she whispers, shaking her head back and forth, her chin wobbling and tears flowing freely down her cheeks.

I stand frozen to the spot, watching her close her eyes in agony, her face contorted in pain. "Our father who art in heaven..." she chokes and swallows hard, "hallowed be thy name..." She grips my St Christopher chain tightly in her hand. Sickness rushes into my throat, but I can't move from this spot. "Finn, please. Finn, I need you please." Her words grip my heart, tightening in my chest, forcing me to surge forward.

I move quickly and take hold of her face. "Angel. It's me; it's Finn. I'm here darlin'..." I don't get to finish before she flies at me, her fists hitting me violently. She's like a wild animal, but one lost in her own world. "Please, I won't tell!" She bangs her fists against my chest.

I pull her toward me and hold her tight, so she can't hurt herself, my heart pounding against her small body, willing her to wake up.

"Angel, Shhh, shhh. It's me darlin'; it's Finn." She shakes her head abruptly, fighting with all her might. I take her palm and flatten it against my heart, covering it with my own.

Her wet face relaxes against my body, and I cradle her in my arms, "Shhh, it's okay, darlin', I got ya. Finns got ya."

She cries softly into my chest, and I don't have a fucking clue if she's awake or not. "The chains they hurt." She holds up her wrist, and I stare at it. Nothing fucking there.

I play along, dread lining my stomach. I gently brush my finger over her wrist. "They're gone darlin'. Gone."

My throat constricts when she whispers the words, "Gone," she repeats it again brokenly.

The door to the room creeps open and Charlie stands in her pink pjs, gripping her teddy by the ear. "Is she okay?" She asks, rubbing the sleep from her eyes.

I swallow hard, knowing I'm lying to my princess. "Yeah.

She's good." I stand with my back to Charlie, covering Angel from her daughter.

Charlie moves closer around the bed and I almost want to shield Angel away to protect them both.

"She didn't take her medication. Should I get it?" I peek down at Angel in confusion. Medication? Glancing back at Charlie, she's stood waiting for a response, so I nod with uncertainty, a grumbling in my chest about not knowing she needed medication, for fuck's sake.

Charlie darts out of the room and I shuffle Angel and me up onto the bed so I can lean against the headboard, cradling her in my arms.

Charlie jumps on the bed without a care in the world. A pile of pill bottles dropped hazardously beside me. I glance back up at Charlie, trying not to let my eyes bug out in shock. She shrugs. "She doesn't like to take them when she's on her own with me." Sighing dramatically, "She said they make her too sleepy." Charlie rolls her eyes. "Then she ends up like this!" she points toward her mama nonchalantly, seemingly unaware of the severity of her mama's terrors.

I glance down at Angel, her eyes wide open, playing with my dog tags, almost in a shock-like state. My throat bobs. "She gets like this a lot?"

Charlie nods a bunch of times, "yep. You have to stroke her hair or her back," she says while shuffling her butt forward and gently stroking Angel's hair from her eyes. "She had a bad time," Charlie coos. I tighten my hold on my girl, giving Charlie a quizzing look. Bad time? What the fuck is she talking about?

"I think someone hurt her. She shouts for you to help. I think it's because you're a soldier, huh? And rescue people, right?" Her dark eyes drill into mine for me to confirm her question. The realization of her words hit me hard, sucking the air from my lungs. Someone hurt her. She begs for me to help. Jesus. I scrub a hand through my hair, my heart crumbling to a thousand pieces, emotion clogs in my throat. Someone hurt my girl.

I can only nod at Charlie, my mind empty of words.

"Will you look after her now? You think you can take away the bad dreams?" Her little hand brushes over Angel's still face. Her eyes are wide open and staring aimlessly into my chest. I swallow away the emotion and kiss Angel on top of her head.

"Yeah, princess, I got her. Both of you. Remember?" I look at her pointedly.

Charlie smiles up at me, my heart hammering at the thought of someone hurting my girls.

"I'm gonna go back to bed. I have camp in the morning," she smiles cheerfully, then shuffles off the bed.

"Night, princess."

"Night, Finn-fitty," she grins.

I stare down at my girl, one hand coiled tightly around the St. Christopher chain, the other clutching my dog tags, her lips moving but her words barely audible. "Give us this day our daily bread." My throat tightens, overcome with emotion. She's chanting the Lord's fucking prayer. Despair and rage course through me. It's clear now someone hurt my girl, hurt her so badly she's terrified to give herself over to me fully. This bastard is keeping my girls from me. My hold tightens, securing her as close as possible. A staggering need of protectiveness engulfs my body, determination setting in. Someone's gonna fucking pay, and when I find out who they are, they'll learn first-hand never to touch what's mine. They'll wish they'd never been born. I'll finish them.

————

I watch her, my eyes never leaving her beautiful face. Questions whirl around in my mind, dread and sympathy encompassing each one of them. She kept my St. Christopher chain, the one I gave her to comfort her when I joined the forces, but I never expected her to need it as a way to comfort her through her nightmares. It was meant to be something to remind her of our future.

I gently trace her tattoos along her delicate arm. The swirl of the rose stems was somewhat soothing. I stop at the motion when I feel a raised, jagged lump; a wave of sickness hits me deep. What the hell? I pull her arm up for closer inspection. Several thick scars in a multitude of lines mar her delicate skin. My stomach turns at the comprehension, my breath stutters. Self-harm, she has tattoos to cover them. Sickness roils in my stomach. She hurt herself? Jesus. What the hell has happened to her?

Angel speaks, her delicate voice barely above a whisper. "I didn't know."

I assess her, scanning over her face, searching for something to tell me she's coherent. "I was pregnant, and I didn't know." She squeezes her eyes shut as if it pains her to remember.

She opens her eyes and watches my hand on her arm, tracing over the scars. She was pregnant when she self-harmed but didn't know she was pregnant? My poor girl, what the hell happened to you?

I lick my lips, my throat suddenly dry. "Someone hurt you, Angel?" She squeezes her eyes shut again, tightly. Her face scrunching up, not wanting to recognize it, she simply nods.

I soothe her, my hand brushing up and down her back. I nuzzle into her hair. Unsure if I'm reassuring her or myself. "It's okay, darlin'. I'm here now. Finn's here." She eases up gently, melting into me, into my arms.

My throat bobs, unsure if to ask the next question or not. I plow on, hoping for more answers. "That's why you ran? Someone hurt you, and you ran?"

She shakes her head, holding out her wrists. But I don't

have a clue what she's trying to tell me, so I just placate her. "This person who hurt you. You scared of him now, darlin'? That why you don't wanna come home?"

Her body jolts below me, a subtle nod leaving her body as she whimpers into my chest. Automatically, my arms tighten around her protectively.

Knowing she's given me enough for now, I let her be. Knowing I'm going to find out who the fuck hurt my girl and make them fucking pay.

They don't call my talent Finn-finishing for no reason. And boy, am I going to enjoy finishing this cunt. I grit my teeth with determination.

CHAPTER 14

Angel

I wake to an excitable little girl bounding on my bed. "Wake up, sleepyhead. It's today. It's camp today!" I smile into Finn's chest, his arm banded tightly around me. I freeze when I realize he's in my bed. Peeking up at him through my lashes, his lazy grin smirks down at me, his head propped up with his arm underneath. Looking hot as hell, I might add. I internally grumble, then chastise myself. Oh shit, he's in my bed.

I had a nightmare! Oh shit, I had a nightmare and Finn is in my bed. I can feel the color drain from my face. "Shh, it's okay, darlin'," he gently coos, stroking my back.

"Can we do pancakes for breakfast?" Charlie smiles, completely oblivious to my panic.

"Yeah, princess. I'm fuckin amazin' at pancakes!"

Charlie gasps wide-eyed at Finn before pointing at him. "Swear jar!"

Finn chuckles, moving me to the side. He shakes his head. "I paid up, remember?"

Charlie wags her finger at him playfully. "You ran out! You have a real bad potty mouth and ran out. Pay up, Mr.

Finn-fitty!" I giggle at their banter; it's adorable. Finn pretends to grumble before feigning reluctance, dragging his hand along the floor to grab his wallet from his jeans and handing over ten dollars.

Charlie is a bundle of energy during breakfast. She adds every topping possible, and I dread to think how her teachers are going to manage the level of hyperactivity.

Finn acts completely unaware of whatever occurred last night, and I'm beyond grateful for that.

Finn

After packing Charlie off and waving her goodbye on the school bus to Camp Wilderness, me and Angel had drinks at a local bar. I was getting fucking pissed at the amount of attention looking her way, checking her out. Is this something she has to deal with on a daily basis? Thank fuck I'm around from now on. My teeth fucking hurt and I'm surprised I haven't shattered a couple from clenching them too hard.

Angel seemed completely unaware, but I saw the fuckers checking my girl's tits out and her hot as fuck ass when she went to the restroom.

Angel chuckled at my annoyance, saying I'm some sort of caveman. I've never chewed through a toothpick so damn quick.

———

Angel busies herself in the kitchen, making us lunch as I sit watching her every move from the kitchen counter, her ass swaying as she works.

The shrill ringing of my cell phone fills the apartment. Angel glances over her shoulder and graces me with a small smile as I make my way over to my phone.

My body tightens with tension. There's only one person who has my number on this phone, Oscar. If he's calling me, then he needs something from me. I grimace at the thought.

I pick up my cell and head toward Angel's bedroom, closing the door behind me so she can't hear.

"Yeah," I answer gruffly.

"You were supposed to check-in," his clipped tone replies.

"You said not to call unless urgent," I reply smugly.

I can hear him fidgeting and his heavy breath breathing out in annoyance. It's so easy to wind Oscar up. "You're needed."

117

My spine tenses, "No."

"Finn. This isn't up for discussion."

I scrub a hand through my hair, panic worrying through me, "Jesus, I said no, Oscar. I've got shit going on here." My eyes glance back at the door.

"Finn, you missed your fight yesterday. That hasn't gone unnoticed. Bren is having a fucking coronary. I can't cover for you much longer."

I lick my lips, my throat dry, panic coursing through me.

Oscar sighs, then continues on. "We've had problems with the shipments again. Security captured one guy, but he isn't saying a word. We need you." He pauses, grimacing the words out, "Your expertise."

I sigh hard, scrubbing a hand through my hair in annoyance. My hands are shaking and my words come out soft and vulnerable. "I can't leave her."

I can almost imagine Oscar nodding in understanding. "Bring her."

I shake my head at him, forgetting he can't see me. "She won't come, Oscar. Shit, there are things I need to discuss with you." My voice rises slightly in panic.

"Bring her!" He cuts the call, and I stare at the screen, pissed and worried. What the fuck am I going to do?

The door creaks open and I raise my head from in between my legs, my arms bracing around my neck. Angel bends down to kneel on the floor between my legs. She gently strokes my back. My anxious eyes meet hers. A small gasp leaves her mouth, worry lining her face. "Wh... what's wrong? What happened?"

I work my throat, knowing I'm about to destroy the trust she has in me. "Oscar." She stills and watches me closely, nodding for me to go on. "He... erm... he needs me back home." I swallow harshly. Her body freezes, and she tries to move away from me. I grip her wrist, stopping her, my palm digging into her tightly. "You're coming with me Angel."

Horror covers her face; her chest rises rapidly; she shakes her head vigorously. "No! No… no way. No, I won't Finn!"

I stroke her wrist, trying to calm her storm. Her legs give way and I jump up to catch her. Cradling her to my chest, she shakes her head back and forth. "No, Finn. I can't. No!"

"Darlin', you can. I swear to fuck you can."

"I'm not. I'll go stay with Chad. Just… just while you're gone."

Rage consumes me. No fucking way. Give her time to leave me? Let her go stay with another guy? Absolutely fucking not.

I grip her chin to look at me, "You're coming, darlin'. Not up for discussion."

Her face crumples, morphing into pain. "Please," she begs. My stomach turns at her plea, knowing what I'm asking of her.

My heart hammers, remembering what Tyler said. "Don't push her. Don't push her away." Anxiety and panic race through me, desperation to keep her. "Just for two nights, Angel." I lick my lips, then go on. "Two fucking nights. I'll… I'll do what I have to do and then we come back here. Or anywhere you fucking want and we start our lives together. Swear it, darlin'. Two nights." And I mean every word. I'll give it all up for her. If that's what she needs, what she wants. She can have Any. Fucking. Thing. My heart races in a panic, desperate for her to agree. "Please," I beg.

She searches my eyes. I feel her relax against me, so I plow on with my plan. "There's only Oscar that knows about you. We stay in my apartment; security is top fucking notch. We stay two nights darlin', then I'm all yours. I'll say goodbye to my life," my throat bobs, "to my family, and I'm yours darlin', just like we wanted. We can go wherever you want." She closes her eyes and clutches my t-shirt as my hand strokes up and down her spine.

"Your… your Ma?" Her lip trembles, her face pained.

"It's okay darlin'. Ma just wants me to be happy. She'll understand." I stroke her hair, knowing I'm winning her over, my racing heart slowing down, "I'll never be happy without you, darlin'. Never. I fucking love you." I sear the words into her eyes, drilling her with the sincerity.

"Two nights." She swallows thickly and agrees with a small reluctant nod, her eyes still wide with uncertainty.

CHAPTER 15

Finn

We drive through the day and into the night, making sure I touch on nightfall as we enter New Jersey. Angel hasn't spoken a word the whole journey, just staring wordlessly out of the window. I've held her hand and drawn circles on her thighs reassuringly. I've attempted to make jokes, started general fuckin' chit-chat. Anything to take her mind away from wherever the fuck it is. But to no avail; she's a shell. I kick myself internally. Am I doing the right thing? Fuck. I pound my hand onto the steering wheel. Her eyes flick toward me. "Are you okay?" Concern laces her voice.

If that's all I needed to do for a reaction, I'd have done it a few fucking hours ago.

I nod and give her a grin. Fake-as-fuck.

She nods and goes back to gazing out into the darkness.

––––––

I pull into the underground parking lot. Fire a text off to Oscar and wait to receive the thumbs up that he's cut the security feed.

"Come on, darlin'." I open my car door and grab the bag from the trunk, moving around to Angel's side. Her door opens, surprising me. Her boots hit the ground, and I track my eyes up to her beautiful face, pale and defenseless. I tug her toward me, drawing her into my arms. Her body comes willingly, and I guide us into the elevator and up to my apartment.

Angel

I follow Finn into his apartment; he explained that his older brother Bren lives in the one above. Con lived below with Will and their son Keen but moved out recently to live in the same gated community as Cal, his wife Lily, and their family.

The apartment is open plan and large, with a minimal and clean-cut feel to it. The marble flooring is white and flows throughout the apartment, which is also very white. I scrunch my nose up at the clinical feel. The kitchen area is also white. My feet move toward the stunning floor-to-ceiling windows that line the back walls of the living area. I stop and almost stumble with the realization someone might see inside. See me.

Completely unaware that Finn has even followed me through the living area, he chuckles beside me awkwardly, his hand resting reassuringly on my lower back. "It's okay darlin'; they're privacy glass so no one can see inside, okay?" He stares at me pointedly and I nod robotically. Still feeling absolutely bewildered and blindsided by being here, a tremble works through my body.

"Come on; I'll show you to our room." My heart melts at his words as I follow him through a door, then down the corridor on the right.

Finn opens the first door and I walk inside, gazing around at the expansive bedroom. A large wooden bed and dressers line the wall. Finn nervously brushes a hand through his hair. "You like?"

My eyes meet his, and I can see the vulnerability in them. I swallow and gently brush my hand down his cheek to his jawline. "It's amazing." His shoulders relax at my comment, and his lip curls into a small smile. I can't help but giggle and chew my lip. He's so sweet sometimes.

"The bathroom's through there," he points to the door nearest to the bed, "the closet in there." His hand waves to a door beside me. "Gonna make yourself at home? I'll go cook something for us, yeah?" I raise my eyebrows. Since when does Finn cook?

His mouth swoops down toward mine, claiming my mouth with his soft lips. I open my mouth for his tongue. Our kiss builds rapidly and becomes aggressive, a mash of tongues and clang of teeth. His hands grip my ass forcefully, all too quickly; he pulls back panting, "fuck darlin'." I grin at myself. "You want me to fuck you? Dirty those clean sheets with your cum?" He glances over my shoulder toward the bed; pristine white sheets lay with zero creases.

I shake my head at him and bite my lip playfully. "No" His eyebrows knit together in confusion, and he scans my face.

Confidently I announce, "I'm going to fuck you!" I smile up at him and push him with a hand on his chest gently toward the bed. This is what I need, the control back.

His heart hammers against my palm, his eyes lighting up at my words. "Fuck yeah, darlin'. You want me naked?" He quizzes eagerly.

I nod, watching as Finn scurries around to the other side of the bed and begins quickly stripping his clothes off. He fumbles at his jeans, then trips over them when he tries to kick them to the side, his face planting into the bed. I splutter a giggle at his eagerness.

Finn jumps back up with a cocky grin and a playful glint in his eye. I scan his body, his gorgeous bronzed abs on full display, his hard erection tenting his boxers. He swiftly pushes them down, leaving him completely bare to me apart from his dog tags.

His cock bobs when he throws himself down on the bed. He cockily pushes his hands to rest under his head and watches me from his pillows with a firm smirk in place.

Agonizingly slow and seductively, without breaking any eye contact, I work my t-shirt over my head; my breasts jiggle as I drop the t-shirt down to the ground. I somehow manage to push down my jeans with grace and step out of them without tripping, leaving me exposed in a skimpy red g-string and matching bra.

Finn's eyes fill with desire, his chest heaving, and his jaw clenching. "Fuck yeah." He moves one hand and begins fisting his cock. I watch as he spreads his pre-cum over the head with his thumb and tugs himself at the base of his cock all the way up to the tip. I clench my thighs together at the sight, my mouth watering for a taste of my man.

I bend down and free myself from my g-string. "Fuck, darlin', really need your pussy up here. Right up here on my cock, darlin'."

I begin a slow crawl up the bed. Finn's eyes not leaving my own; they briefly flick down to my heaving breasts and then back up. Hunger and desperation seeping through his stare. He rises up from the pillow and moves closer to me.

His mouth parts slightly as I reach his crotch. I swoop down and swirl my tongue around his balls. He sucks in a loud, audible breath as I trail my tongue up his shaft. He holds his cock firmly in his hand, his body filled with tension as he watches me drench his cock with my tongue and finally to his thumb resting on the head of his cock, his voice heady and full of lust. "Lick the slit, darlin', lick it good." I push my tongue into his slit, his gaze unwavering. I swirl it around the head and dip it once again into the slit. "Holy fuckin' hell. Fuck darlin', I wanna cum all fuckin' over you." I pull back with a cheeky grin. Finn instantly sags with disappointment.

"Lay back, Finn." He does as instructed instantly, quickly laying back onto the pillow, his hand leaving his hardness.

"You want me to be a dirty, Angel?" I ask with the cock of my brow, trailing my tongue over my lip before plucking it into my mouth. Finn's eyes light with fire, his dark, intense gaze tracking my every movement. "Dirty, darlin', so damn dirty. I'm gonna need mother fucking cleansing after you're done with me."

I glance around the room, "do you have a tie?"

Finn tilts his head to the dresser. "Over there, top drawer."

I strut back over to the bed with the tie dangling in one hand and a thin bottle of lube in my other. I motion with my head toward the bed frame. "Hands up." Finn's cocky smile encompasses his face.

"Gotta say, darlin', never been tied up before." He grins.

I stare down at Finn as I tie his hands to the headboard, my body straddling his, my tits bouncing near his head, his eyelids heavy with lust.

I shuffle back on my knees and without giving either of us a chance to think, I take hold of his cock and line him up, slamming down on him aggressively. The breath is sucked from my lungs, his thickness stretching me deliciously. "Oh fuck, that's good, Finn!" My mouth drops open at the feeling of being filled with his cock.

Finn's mouth is open in awe. He swallows harshly. "Again. Fucking fuck me, Angel," he chokes the words out. I lift and slam myself down on him. Over and over, my tits bounce and Finn's eyes track them. I squeeze them seductively as I roll my hips over his waist, my clit loving the feel of his rough skin beneath me. I pluck at my nipples, causing my pussy to clench. "Oh, fuck, Angel!"

Bending my head, I swipe my tongue into his open mouth; my pussy squeezes around him; causing him to groan. "Need to taste your nipples, darlin'." I grip my breast and feed it into his open mouth. He mumbles incoherent words, and a "fuck," escapes him while I swirl my hips over and over, my body bent to accommodate his filled mouth. His tongue plucks my nipple into a peak and he sucks gently around my piercing, the feeling like no other. The wetness runs down my leg as I moan desperately, eager, for more. I slow my movements, embracing the feel of his tongue playing with my nipple.

I pull back from him, my nipple popping from his mouth. Finn watches me with desire-filled eyes. I flip the cap off the lube, squirting some into my palms. I lean back on an arm, my body now stretching backward. Finn's eyes trail over me before moving back down to where we are joined, his cock moving deliciously slowly in and out of my wet pussy. He gasps for breath as he pushes into me again.

I used my free hand to massage his balls before moving closer to his ass. "Angel?" Finn questions.

"Relax, you'll love it." I smile back at him. Before he has a chance to reply, I push my finger into his asshole and head straight for his g spot. Finn's ass lifts off the bed with my sudden movement and a loud groan escapes him; his tussled fists clench and unclench. "Holy. Holy fuck. Fuuuuckkk," he screeches and hammers into me as I thrust my finger in and out of his ass, taking care to massage around his rim with my thumb. The movement makes Finn buck wildly, his hips lifting off the bed and his cock pistoling in and out of me.

The stretch of my pussy and the force of his thrusts make me desperate to release. "Oh fuck, Finn. Come. Please come." I beg, feeling my own orgasm take over. I can feel him swell inside me, and my pussy contracts and milks him as waves upon waves of pleasure float through my body.

My body drops lax on top of Finn's, completely spent and dazed from the amazing orgasm we've both just encountered.

CHAPTER 16

Finn

After being fucked within an inch of my life and left with a raw fucking cock and delicate ass, I made me and Angel pasta. I took note that my girl hadn't eaten all day, and that's not something I'm gonna stand for. She needs looking after, that's for sure.

I let her take back control today in the bedroom. For the first time in my life, I let someone control me. I knew how vulnerable Angel felt, so giving her this was something that benefited us both because, honestly, that thing she did with my ass was Mother. Fucking. Awesome. I don't even want to know where she learned it but fuck it was incredible. I came seeing stars with my girl riding me like I was a fucking stallion.

I kiss Angel goodnight and reassure her for the thousandth time that nobody knows she's here. She has her cell phone to contact me in an emergency, and I also slipped some of her sleeping pills into her meal to make sure she's relaxed and asleep while I'm at this meeting with my brothers. It was the kindest thing to do for her.

I finally pull up to our warehouse, careful to take note of who is on security and where they are situated, again something from the Army that never leaves me. I take a deep breath and stroll toward the main doors. Sam, one of our security details, greets me at the main door. "Evening, Sir, they're in Bren's office." I nod in response and walk through the door he now holds open.

I religiously scan the area for threats, even though I know Oscar has security wrapped up pretty god damn tight.

I can hear my brothers before I even see them. A sense of calm and comfort wrap around my hardened heart. The only time I ever feel more at ease is when I'm with Angel. A feeling of dread at leaving them behind makes my heart skip a beat.

Shaking myself up, I open the door and stride inside.

"Just where the fuck have you been?" Bren's voice bellows, bringing me back down to earth with a fucking bump. I mask my features and pull on my badass attitude they know all too well. All my brothers' heads turn in my direction, awaiting a response.

I shrug nonchalantly and drop into the chair beside Oscar, opening my legs wide and shoving a fresh toothpick into my mouth. Bren's fist hits the table hard, making the table ricochet with the force. "I asked you a goddamn question!"

Con's eyes dart up from his phone. Appearing a tad bit pissed, Bren interrupted whatever the fuck he was doing on it.

I sigh, "I had shit to do, Bren."

Bren's eyes narrow and scan my body and then search furtively over my face. I stare back at him with an air of confidence I don't actually feel. His shoulders are tense as he watches me for what I'm not sure. Does he know? "You missed your fight," his voice sounds slightly concerned at my odd behavior.

I glance away. "Yeah, I had shit to do."

"Who?" Con's eyebrows dance playfully, and I smirk at him knowingly.

"You went fucking AWOL over a woman? I've had Don chewing my ass out over you not fighting Saturday night!" Bren spews, anger radiating off of him. His nostrils flare, and his neck veins protrude. So that's why he's pissed? Because I missed an underground fight?

"I deserve a fucking day off, Bren!" I bite back.

Bren breathes in deeply, so fucking deep the entire table goes still and waits for his response. His chest rises and I swear the buttons on his shirt look like they're gonna pop open and that's not just with the muscle. I scrub a hand through my hair uncomfortably. His teeth bite into his lower lip, and his fists flex on the table. "Gonna fuck you up in a minute, motherfucker!" Bren's eyes drill into me, making me squirm in my seat.

"If you can stop acting like a damn Neanderthal for two minutes, I'd like to proceed with today's meeting. I have things that need attending to…" Oscar chimes in, in his usual patronizing tone. Thankfully breaking the tension like a saint, fuck, I love my brother.

"I bet I know what you need attending to…" Con quips back, his eyebrows overtly dancing, "Am I right?" He gestures toward Oscar's crotch.

Oscar sneers at him, complete disgust was written all over his face, "How in the hell Will puts up with your immature ass, I don't know." He glares at Con as though he's shit on his shoe.

"She loves me." Con's face is alight with fucking glee. He even leans forward, elbow on the table and resting his head on his fist like some lovesick puppy.

Cal clears his throat. "Anyway, carry on Oscar…"

"Yes. Thank you, Cal," he nods his thanks toward Cal and continues on, "As you all know, we've had two missing shipments this month. This isn't the first time. However, this month it's been a lot more blatant. It was done by someone on the inside. I scanned back over the security footage and caught a member of staff selecting cargo. They just so happen to be the cargo that goes missing on route to their location."

"How exactly do you mean select?" Cal asks, sitting forward in his chair.

"He went through the paperwork as he should, but the cameras caught him putting a blue sticker on the cargo crates that just so happen to be the ones that then go missing. That's how I realized it was him."

"Where is he now?" I ask, anger racing through me at the disrespectful prick that's been stealing from us.

"He's in the basement. I roughed him up, but he's saying fuck all." Bren stares back at me with venom in his eyes; his thick finger points at me. "Could have done with you yesterday. When we caught the fucker! What if whoever he's in contact with has been alerted to him going missing, huh?" The tendons in his neck stick out through his shirt. Fuck, he's seething.

I sag in my chair. Bren's right; I should have been here. My stomach churns at the realization that I'm needed here just as much as I'm needed with Angel. Something's got to give.

I'm going to disappoint someone, correction, more than one because either way, there's more than just one person involved. My heart hammers at the thought of hurting any of them, a dull ache threatening to tear open with the revelation bound to tear us all apart. I rub my hand over the pain in my chest, willing it away.

My eyes catch on to Cal's, his boring into mine with scrutiny. "Nice nails," as he tips his head toward where my hands are steepled in front of me. My heart hammers in my chest when I glance down at my multicolored, glittered nails courtesy of my princess.

Con stifles a laugh with his fist in his mouth. Cocky little fucker. I don't even chance a glance in Bren's direction. I can feel the heat and rage radiating from him. "If I were you, I'd take her to Prim and Polished downtown. They're amazing with kids. Honestly, I took Chloe, and she actually sat babbling to the beautician while she painted her nails this cute, soft pink. They matched her dress perfectly." Cal smiles to himself, recalling his trip to a fucking nail salon. His hands are all animated as he speaks; who the fuck is he? Where the hell is my brooding, serious brother?

"You're dating?" Bren asks, intrigue laced in his tone.

The pain in my chest worsens. "No." I clip back quickly, too fucking quickly.

"She has a kid?" Cal asks, gesturing once again toward my hands that are now turning into fists, my teeth grinding in annoyance at their intruding questions.

"Can we get back to the meeting?" Oscar prompts, saving the fucking day.

Bren straightens, his arrogant head of the family swiftly back in place. "This Deacon guy, what exactly do we know?"

Oscar's eyes scan the table to make sure he has all our attention. "So Deacon Jessop has worked in our warehouse for a little under three years, a petty criminal with no connections that I can find to any other organized group. I have managed to track down a bank account that money was paid into on a monthly basis, but there's no trace of where it came from."

"What about his phone records?" Cal asks.

Oscar nods. "Again, no trace of where the messages he received came from. Whoever he is involved with are covering their tracks well. That in itself is rather worrying. A small-time gang would not be able to cover anything from me."

You can feel the aggression rolling off Bren. His neck is so fucking tight it's a wonder he doesn't choke himself with his own thick veins.

Con's loud chuckle breaks through the growing tension. Bren's head swivels aggressively in Con's direction.

Con holds his hands up in defense, "I'm sorry, proud fucking daddy right here!" His broad grin lighting up his face, he holds his phone up in his hand as if he's showing us a trophy.

Bren's shoulders dip slightly at the mention of our brother being a daddy and whatever the fuck Keen has done to make him so damn proud.

Con goes on to explain his excitement, "It's Peppa; he's shit outside again," he smiles widely, holding up three fingers, "Three fucking days in a row man! We've nailed it! Fucking nailed it, I tell ya!" His smug grin and admittance make him sit straighter with pride oozing from him.

Our mouths drop open one by one.

Con's eyes scan our faces, completely oblivious to our reactions but expecting us to be as equally overjoyed.

"You interrupted a mother fucking meeting to tell us your damn bold cunt of a dog shit outside?!" Bren's exasperated face mortifies with rage.

Con's eyebrows furrow in confusion. I mean, did he seriously expect us to be happy? His jaw tics, and his eyes turn harsh, "Don't fucking call my dog a cunt! Why the fuck you got to be such a prick, huh?"

"He needs to get laid." I chime in, just because.

Bren's manic eyes swivel between mine and Con's as if struggling to rein in control and decide who he's going to make suffer first.

Oscar clears his throat, his voice high and demanding, "Have we quite finished?" We all turn our attention to Oscar. He glances down at his tablet and then continues, "Deacon Jessop is in the basement awaiting your expertise, Finn." His eyes drill into me pointedly. "We need to know where the shipment was going to and who his contacts are." I tilt my head in acknowledgment.

133

I jump up from my chair and clap my hands together, "Let's get this mother fucking party started then."

CHAPTER 17

Finn

My boots hit the concrete with a clunk as we descend the stone stairs one by one.

The pungent smell of piss fills my nostrils and feeds my need for vengeance. No fucker steals from us and gets away with it. This fucker is going to pay today with his life. I lick my lips in anticipation; my whole muscles flex with the thoughts of relieving some of my growing tension.

Cal throws himself lazily into a chair. Oscar steps into the corner of the room, silently overseeing and assessing. Bren stands stoically beside me while Con bounces on his feet like an excitable child, touching all my tools.

I'm fully aware of how fucked up our family is, but it's our fucked up, and I'm good with that.

The dude, Deacon Jessop, stirs in his chair when he hears us. I step forward. His eyes flare with sheer panic at the recognition of my face. He tugs at his restraints desperately, "Pp… please I. I don't know anything, I swear!" His mouth agape.

I take the scalpel from Con and swirl it around in my hand haphazardly. "I see you've heard of me?" I quiz with glee.

The dude swallows thickly, his busted lip trembles. I take in his body and recognize several injuries caused by Bren. The broken cheekbone, misplaced shoulder, snapped fingers, probably leg too, given how askew it sits. Mmm, I can do better, I ponder; I scrub a hand over my jaw. Much better.

His legs begin to shake as if hearing my thoughts. I meet his eyes from under my dark lashes.

His mouth drops open with terror. I'm unsure what he sees, but I know how I feel. The darkness has consumed me, a nagging open-pore desperate to be fed.

"Do you know what they call my skill set?" I ask darkly, tilting my head from side to side. I slash into the palm of my own hand, embracing the feeling of release, the endorphins pulsating out of the open wound. The dude stares at me in sheer horror, frozen to the core.

I move toward him, his gaze was unwavering, still as a statue. Clearly, he's in some state of shock. Lucky for me, I know just how to get him out of his hypnotic state.

I smear the blood from my palm over his face, and the dude doesn't bat an eye, consumed with terror. I chuckle and step backward, allowing Con to step forward intuitively. Con nods toward Cal, who walks forward and proceeds to turn on the hose.

The ice-cold water sprays over the top of Deacon's head, his body jolts in shock before the shakes set in. His eyes catch mine through the flood of water being dumped over his broken body.

Con chuckles at Deacon's reaction, moving away once again and allowing me to continue. "They call what I do, Finn-finishing. Do you know why?" I ask mockingly.

"Yy… yo… you finish them?" He stutters.

I shake my head, dropping it in disappointment. "No," my palms twitch, "I give them a finishing touch before finishing them!" I correct him, both anger and glee seeping through my veins. Why do they always get it fucking wrong? My fists clench in annoyance.

"Now, Deacon Jessop, I can do this the easy way or the hard way. You will tell me everything. Do you understand me?"

The fear radiates from him. He nods up and down like a puppet. His eyes never leaving mine, almost glued to my movements.

"Now, who do you work for?"

He shakes his head desperately.

I move swiftly; before Deacon can bat a fucking eye, my fingers find his nostrils and pull his head sideways violently. "You seem to have problems with your hearing. You won't be needing this," I slice down his face, cutting into just above his ear, gauging my scalpel in and yanking the flesh from his head. I tear off his ear. His screams vibrate off the walls, his feet hopelessly drag onto the floor in a desperate and feeble attempt to stand.

His thick blood pools down his disfigured face. I drop the ear into the blood-stained bowl that Con is holding out toward me.

"Strip him!" I point my scalpel in Bren's direction. He nods and moves forward, opening his own knife.

"NO! No, please. No. I'll speak! I swear I'll speak."

Bren ignores his hopeless pleas and cuts his clothes swiftly from his crumbling body.

My eyes catch Oscar, his own eyes transfixed in fascination at the show before him.

"Now, Deacon. Left or right?" I motion to each side of him with my hand.

Deacon's eyes flit between me and my brothers in confusion.

My head tilts with ridicule. "Left or right?" I point my scalpel toward his limp cock and balls. His face falls once again, a grimace taking over, then the dude tries to expel his stomach. I stroke my jaw and patiently await for his melt-down to subside.

"I... I was approached by someone... th... they said that if I did this for them, they would pay me and if I told you, they'd hurt my family. I... I didn't have a choice!"

Con hands me the pliers, and I move forward.

"Jesus!" Cal breathes out. I hear him shuffle behind me, the movement causing my mouth to curl in approval. He's such a pussy.

I grip the pliers and advance on Deacon; his body flays pathetically, attempting to shrink away from me. The thought makes me chuckle.

I almost wince when I clasp his shriveled ball into the vise-like gripper. I snip and step back to watch the blood transcend from his body. A deafening shriek fills my ears before the inevitable silence. His head lolls forwards. I drop the ball into the awaiting bowl.

I sigh and motion with my hand for Con to conduct the next procedure. He jabs the needle into the dude's thigh brutally without the usual care you'd expect when administering.

Deacon gasps, his head snaps up, his eyes shooting open and straight into my own, manically waiting.

He quickly peeks down at his dick and one ball, then back up at me, blood pooling around him. "They paid me once every two weeks." His voice shakes. "Into a new account. I don't know where the money came from. I have a bit of a habit and needed the cash." So the dude's into drugs? "I didn't even know the guy that approached me. I swear." He rambles, no doubt telling me everything Oscar knows already. Of course, he'll have checked into Deacon's accounts.

"You said they?" Oscar steps forward from the shadows.

Deacon nods continuously, "The… the guy who approached me said someone would text me instructions."

"What were the instructions?" Oscar asks.

"They… they said to change the stickers on the shipments. That they'd text me which ones the night before. The new stickers were posted at my apartment. That's it man, I swear! That's all I know!" His eyes implore at my nonexistent conscience as I brush off his attempts.

"Please!" he begs. Snot dripping from his nose and wetness dripping from his busted eyes. His whole-body now shaking with exposure to the shock, pain, and coldness.

"Did you take any of our drugs, Deacon?" My bitter voice asks.

His eyes flick around the room with terror.

"My family. They're innocent in all of this. Please don't let them get hurt. Pl… please." I sneer in his direction, hating the begging and mention of family. They always mention the family. "I have a bit of a habit. I said I'd do this, and they'd pay me."

"Did you steal drugs from us, too?" I ask again.

His chest rises and falls in panic. "Maybe once or twice."

I nod toward Con. He brings the bowl forward. "Wha… what are you going to do with them?" his whole-body vibrates.

"Dinner time, my friend. Dinner time." I revel in his visibly mortified discomfort.

Bren rolls up his sleeves and moves forward. He forces Deacon's mouth open, almost breaking his jaw in the process; Bren's huge hands clutch Deacon's jaw in a vise-like grip.

"That's it. I'm out. I'm fucking out!" Cal screeches from behind, throwing his hands up like a toddler.

"Stand fucking down!" Bren snaps in Cal's direction at his pussy ass attitude. He's meant to be next in command after Bren, for Christ's sake. Cal skulks back over to his chair, grumbling and grimacing like a petulant child.

Deacon struggles and tries hopelessly to expel the body parts from his throat. He gags, but Bren snaps his jaw shut with a firm grasp, holding it in place. Deacon's head flings from side to side, convulsing aimlessly.

"Are we finishing him?" Con asks while cleaning his fingernails with a scalpel.

Deacon's eyes flare like a goddamn coward. At least take it like a man, dude. "Of course, we're finishing him," I look at my brother pointedly. "It's what I do best!" I grin.

CHAPTER 18

Finn

I slip into bed beside Angel. After a shower to wash away the blood and grime from obliterating the last bit of life from that shit bag, Deacon. I cut him up enough to squeeze him into a steel container and fill it with acid, knowing before long, any trace of him would be liquefied. We shipped him off on a brief trip across the Hudson River, where he'll be deposited into the ocean, no doubt eventually leaking into the seabed and becoming the bottom feeder he always was.

I snuggle down deeper into my bed and tug my girl into the crook of my arm. Her strawberry smell wraps around me, encompassing me with warmth, a far cry from the sickness and rage inside me earlier. Now ease fills me, settling my mind and body. I embrace the feeling of another side of me, the side reserved for Angel and our princess.

Breathing in her familiar scent, I close my eyes, considering myself the luckiest motherfucker to walk this earth. I have the love of my life in bed with me, and nothing can take her away from me. I slowly drift off to sleep, my heavy eyes giving in to the flood of exhaustion running through my body.

Angel stirs gently, a whimper shooting me awake.

A deep-seated pit of dread enters my body. A reminder of the damage caused to my girl, my innocent, sweet girl. The thrum of my own heart can be heard as I squeeze her reassuringly tighter toward me. My arms banding possessively around her.

A harsh reminder I have to speak to Oscar. There's shit to resolve.

Before we start our new life, I need to abolish the old one.

Angel

I stir slowly, my head feeling somewhat cloudy. I tug the sheets off of me with a groan. The light streaming through the blinds into the room is the only sign that I slept through the night. I scrub a hand through my wayward hair and make my way into the bathroom to freshen up. Squinting up toward the mirror, I try not to acknowledge the redness under my eyes or the anxious gleam in them. Ignoring the nauseating feeling of dread just being here as I scrub my teeth to freshen my dry throat. I stand straighter and prep myself. Just today, then we're gone, and we don't have to return. Ever.

Even as I tell myself this, I know it's a lie. I can feel it deep inside. An overwhelming anxious ball of dread escalates with every minute we're here. In this town. This apartment. I will myself forward. For Finn's sake, I make my way into the kitchen.

———

His toned muscled back is on full display as he stirs something on the stove. I bite my lip as I watch my gorgeous guy practically dance around the kitchen cooking, his head bopping along to some song playing low on the radio. His gray joggers land precariously low on his waistline, his toned ass encasing them perfectly. I smile internally at how insanely hot he is, and he's mine. All freaking mine.

Finn clears his throat. My eyes travel up to see him peering over his shoulder at me, his deep blue eyes dancing with jest. His eyes dip down to my mouth, and a cocky smirk graces his face. "Come here."

I swing my hips, slowly walking over to him. He clicks the switch on the stove and turns to fully face me, giving me his full attention. He leans back against the cupboard with his arms stretched on either side, his hands resting on the countertop, his legs stand apart. My eyes travel the span of his body, stopping on his cock, his thickness protruding against the joggers. My mouth waters at the sight of him. My legs have a mind of their own and stand between his. His gaze causes my nipples to pebble through my thin cami top at his intense stare. My thighs squeeze together, the moisture seeping through my panties. I want him; I want him so fucking bad.

Finn's Adam's apple bobs as he takes me in. "Mmm, I can smell your pussy, Angel." I gasp at his crude words, a combination of shock and arousal. I lick my lips in response.

Finn's eyes flick to the side, and mine follow. His leather jacket lays slung on one of the bar chairs. He grins. "Undress, Angel, I'm going to fuck you in my jacket." A smile tugs at my lips. Imagining his scent and the roughness of his jacket surrounding me while he pounds into me makes me work my panties down with haste.

I fling my top over my head and stand before Finn, completely naked; he drops his pants and stands like a fucking sex god baring all to me. He tugs aggressively on his cock, a sheer coating of cum marring the tip. I moan at the sight, my heart racing.

I grab Finn's jacket and tug it on; it's big, too big. But I love it, the feel, the weight, the scent. I love everything about it; it's Finn. "Fuck, darlin'," his voice is coated in lust. He moves forward and picks me up, placing me on the counter.

His lips dip in for a kiss, his length pushed against my thigh, I wiggle to relieve the throb between my legs, Finn chuckles and moves back slightly, gazing down at me with pure desire in his eyes; his hands move toward my neck, and I lower my brows in confusion. He unclasps the St Christopher cross necklace from around my neck and places it on the counter, then he unhooks his dog tags and places them over my neck, the weight of them dangling between my heavy breasts.

His gaze meets mine, and he swallows thickly, "You're my girl, Angel." I nod my head and curl my arms around his neck, pulling him closer, desperately closer. My lips hit his, and his tongue weaves into my mouth. My body tingles with desire. One arm grasps around to my ass and pulls me closer. I open my legs wider to accommodate him between my legs, his hand grips his cock, and he strokes the head through my folds, "Ah Finn, please," moans escape me, and I clench my pussy willing his cock to enter me. "Pl… please," I beg.

Finn bites his lip and sinks into me agonizingly slow. "That's it darlin', take my cock." I nod as I feel the push of his hard thickness stretching me, painfully slow as his free hand grips my thigh as if steadying himself, holding himself back.

The tight grip on my thigh is almost punishing me for his own steady pace. I'm loving the eagerness of his grip, his desperation, a clear sign he's struggling to maintain the slow-ness. A tremble escapes me when Finn bottoms out and hits the perfect spot. "Finn," I gasp; I draw his head closer to mine for me to capture his soft lips. "Please," he pulls back. Then slams into me. If his grip wasn't bruising tight, I would be halfway across the counter with the force. He repeats the motion, driving his hips rapidly into my own.

Finn's eyes dart to the side and his pupils dilate. He grabs the item. Holding up a bottle of oil, he pulls the cap off with his teeth; I watch as he pours the contents down my throat, a gasp leaving my open mouth as the trail flows between my breasts and down to where we're joined. "Fuuuckkk," Finn chokes when the liquid hits his cock. "Darlin'," his eyes meet mine. I instantly let go of his neck and open the jacket to give Finn a better view of my tits. The oozing liquid runs greasily around them, pooling at our sex.

Finn's eyes don't leave my own, watching me through a haze as I smear the oil over my breasts, tugging and squeezing the peaks. "Sweet fucking Jesus, that's hot!" His mouth opens in awe, his cock throbbing deep inside me. He begins to move, but his eyes remain on my breasts. "Don't stop darlin', play with those tits. Don't fucking stop." He hammers into me. I grip his head and push them toward my tits, desperate to feel his mouth around my nipples, his wet tongue over them.

He pulls one into his mouth and sucks and sucks. "Oh, shit!"

"I know darlin', fuck!" He thrusts. "Grip," thrust. "My," thrust. "Cock, darlin'." I don't need him to tell me. I'm already squeezing him in a vise-like grip as my orgasm hits with the thrust of his pelvis, hitting my engorged clit.

Finn's mouth becomes animalistic, biting, grabbing, sucking, and licking my breasts with sheer desperation. I claw at his back, my nails are sure to draw blood. "Fiiinnnn," I screech as I climax around his length. I feel the swell of his cock, and I revel in it. I scream for it, "Come, Finn. Cum inside me!"

"Fuckkkk, Angel. Fucking take it." His hips stutter and he groans, his mouth clutching at my breast stills, pulling at the skin between his teeth, marking me. I feel him the moment his cum floods my womb; I sink into the sensation, the high and feel of him coating me inside and marking me outside.

Slowly Finn looks up at me, his mouth still parted, a sheen of sweat glistening his forehead. His lips dip gently to mine, a stark contrast from only moments ago when he was eager to ruin my body. He pulls back slightly, "say it," his eyes vulnerably searching mine, and he waits stoically still for my response, uncertainty coating his entire demeanor.

A small smile tugs at my lips at his soft actions. I meet his eyes with ease, the confidence in my words oozing from me, "I love you." His whole-body relaxes, and he sags into me; his hand softly cups my jaw. "Love you too, darlin'." I grin at his words and kiss his lips.

"Pretty sure I fucked a baby into you." He smirks at me, waiting for a response.

I roll my eyes, "pretty sure I need to get on birth control."

He ducks his head down and nips at the skin on my neck. "Like fuck you are. I'm keeping ya. You and my baby." His eyes dart down at my stomach, and I push at him playfully.

Finn backs away, making me instantly feel the loss of his body. "Go shower, I'll erm," his eyes dart around the kitchen, "tidy round and salvage breakfast." His eyebrows shoot up at the mess created. I giggle softly and nod; my feet touch the slippery floor and I give my ass an extra wiggle as I walk away.

"Gonna use that oil to fuck that ass, Angel." Finn shouts at my retreating back as I make my way toward the door.

"I'm counting on it, Finn!" I grin back without turning around.

I can hear him laugh as I step into his room. My mood completely changed from when I was last in here. That's what Finn does to me; he has the capability of making me happy. Making me, me again. A warmness settles in my heart.

One more day to go.

CHAPTER 19

inn

After I pull on my joggers, I mop the floor and wipe the surfaces, all the while my smile is securely in place on my usual subdued face. The way Angel makes me feel is an invincible force of happiness I otherwise never would know existed. The thought of her carrying my baby makes me want to shout to the world, "I got my family!"

The doorbell chimes, and I freeze at the sound, instantly on alert for whoever is visiting my door. My eyebrows furrow as I quickly try to gauge who it could be. I've seen my brothers, so I'm not sure why any of them would come around. They barely do anyway. There's only a handful of people who would have been able to gain entry to my apartment this far, and none of them are a threat. I listen instinctively for the sound of the shower running and, on confirmation that it is, I walk over to the security screen by the door.

My uncle Don's face, fills the screen, his broad shoulders tense in his usual stoic stance. I sigh and run a palm over my jaw; this is going to be hard fucking work. My mood instantly plummets.

I open the door and wait for the tongue lashing that is bound to follow.

His dark eyes drill into mine, fury and violence consuming them, my shoulders slacken in guilt. "Where the feck have you been?" He spits out, literally spits out. I almost want to wipe it from my chest, but I don't want to piss him off any more than necessary.

"Lost your feckin tongue?" His nostrils flare in rage at my lack of response.

I sigh, "I... I was out of town," shit, I brush my hand through my hair.

Don pushes past me and barges into the apartment. My body freezes at his actions. "I'll ask you again, Finn. Where the feck were ya?" His fists clench beside him.

I swallow, not wanting to lie to my uncle but at the same time knowing I need to continue this pretense. "I was in Long Island they hold Dambe tournaments in some of the underground scenes; I was checking them out." I shrug nonchalantly.

He's watching me closely, calculating and assessing me. "Dambe?"

I nod and duck my head, hoping to disguise the heavy swallow. "Yeah, Dambe."

"You planning on branching out?" His eyes light up with glee. I already have an excellent reputation as a street fighter.

I shrug again. "Maybe."

He nods in slow acknowledgment of my words, probably seeing the dollar signs behind his lids.

"You missed your fight Saturday night, Finn." He stares at me pointedly. "You made us appear fucking weak. My own fighter, my own nephew. A feckin no show!" His voice gets louder, and my chest rises with panic. Thankfully, I can still hear the shower running. Now I need to get him out of here before Angel finishes in the bathroom.

"I know. I'll pay you back. It was an opportunity that couldn't be missed." I meet his eyes and hold his, hoping he can't see through the lie.

He ducks his head, "Yeah, you feckin will pay me back, little shite." He mumbles the latter part, and I know I've won him over.

Slowly, Don walks toward the door before turning around and stopping to face me down. "Bring ya self a prize back?" He throws his head toward the bedroom and the noise of the shower. His eyes alight with his own joke.

I nervously fake a laugh, "Yeah, something like that." Don watches me closely as if he can smell the lie; his eyes penetrate through me, pulling the truth from behind the facade. Then, without warning, he releases them, his eyes darting around the room. Looking for something? Something out of place. My own eyes follow his, quicker, desperate to make sure there's no evidence of my visitor. His eyes are still, and his body winds tight, but he's staring at the empty kitchen counter. Fucking weird.

Then he turns his back and walks through the door without another word said.

The door clasps shut and my body sags against it, the tension still winding my muscles tight. Fuck. I bang my head against the door in annoyance with myself and the situation. My eyes catch onto a small shimmer on the countertop, and I realize it's Angel's St Christopher chain sitting there, shining at me like a beacon. A sickness I don't recognize works its way up inside me. Where the fuck did this feeling come from? I shake my head at my own ridiculous body betraying me.

I glance down the hallway to where Angel is still in the shower.

I push off the wall and stroll down the hallway. When I slowly ease open the bedroom door, a sudden reality hits me. The shower is running, but not once has there been a break in the water? It's been continuous. My legs work quickly, tearing open the bathroom door in a panic to see what has happened to Angel.

The room is steaming, and I open the shower door expecting to find my girl, but it's empty. I switch off the shower and scan the room before moving back into the bedroom. Again, a wave of sickness hits me, bringing me to a standstill. What the fuck is happening?

Low murmuring enters my ears; I stand still and listen for the sound and realize it's coming from my closet.

I gently open the door and my eyes dart down to the broken girl at my feet. I can feel my breath caught in my throat, the harsh hammer of my heart against my chest, my legs wobble at the sight of Angel in a fetal position, clutching at my dog tags. "Our father, who art in heaven…" her sobs consume her.

I kneel down and speak low, "Angel, Angel darlin', can you hear me?"

Angel gasps and begins clutching her throat, making a gut-wrenching choking sound. Panic races through me. "Shit, Angel, breathe. Can you breathe?" Nothing, she sucks in air and chokes, her whole-body shaking worryingly, dangerously shaking. The choking gets louder, her eyes wide with fear but completely unaware of her surroundings. She stills, taking my heart with hers, plummeting to the ground and crashing.

"Ang… Angel?" I try to soothe her, stroke her hair. There's nothing. She doesn't so much as blink. She's lifeless. My hand trembles against her throat as I check for a pulse. I swallow deeply, unsure if it's my own pulse or hers I can feel. Fear, complete and utter fear, "Jesus." I pull her into my arms and stand with her, her body a dead weight, cold and completely lifeless. I march toward the living area, pulling my phone from my pocket and fumbling with it. I manage to press one. "Oscar… Oscar, I need help. Please, fuck, I need help. It's

Angel, please." My voice breaks, unable to hold myself together any longer. "Please."

I drop to the couch with my girl curled into me, cradling her like a baby. I kiss her forehead. "Please, Angel. Please wake up for me darlin'." A tear falls from my eyes, hitting her cheek. I just need someone to help her. Please.

CHAPTER 20

Angel

I bounce on my feet into the bathroom and start the shower. I'm giddy with excitement. Our new start is only a stone's throw away. I step into the warm water and lather my body, breaking through the oil with the loofah and body wash I scrub while biting my lip at the memories encompassing me. Wetness pools between my thighs. I glance toward the door when an idea springs to mind. I smile to myself and step out of the shower. Finn could sure use a shower right now, too. Screw breakfast.

I grab Finn's t-shirt off of the counter and cover myself, smiling at my idea as I make my way through the bedroom, my hand clasped on the door handle. I realize I can hear voices, raised voices.

"Yeah, Dambe."

"You planning on branching out?" His voice cuts through my heart, my whole-body gasps, my hand trembles on the door handle, panic races into my throat, clogging the air.

Every nerve in my body screams at me to do something. I want to yell, shout something, anything. Nothing moves; I can't breathe. I choke on my own breath, my throat paralyzed. I fall to my knees, consumed by sheer terror.

My mouth is wide open, fighting for air. I struggle to even move. I try to crawl, but my body has a mind of its own, shaking and wobbling. My vision becoming hazy, his voice playing over in my head, scaring me, consuming me. Coming for me. I slowly get my body to do what I want, to getaway. One fist at a time, I claw at the floor and crawl. My throat constricts as I try desperately to breathe again.

I crawl on my hands and knees, stumbling and struggling to keep upright on all fours. I somehow manage to get into the closet, into a dark space, a safe space. Away from the voice, the one in my nightmares.

I reach for my cross and find Finn's dog tags. My Finn. I close my eyes tightly and begin to recite a prayer. Praying for the voices to go away, the pain to go away. Him to go away.

"On earth as it is in heaven." I squeeze my eyes shut.

My body is shutting down, my mind taking over.

My body curled tight with fear.

Finn

The door to the apartment flies open, with Oscar leading my brothers, Bren and Cal, into the room with haste.

My eyes dart to Oscar's in desperation. His clipped voice comes out, "What's wrong with her?"

"I... I... I don't know. I went to check on her in the shower, and I found her in the closet like this," I stutter over my words as Oscar kneels before me and begins checking Angel's responses.

"Is that?" My eyes meet Cal's, his laced in shock.

"Fuckin', Jesus, what the hell happened to her, Finn?" Bren's wide eyes meet mine. "She's..." he waves his hands in Angel's direction. His eyes traveling over her body, her tattoos, hair, and piercings, his eyes getting unbelievably wider by the second.

"Different," Cal finishes for him, his voice a soft whisper. I just nod in response to them. I don't care if she's different; she's fucking mine. My arm tightens protectively around her.

"Finn, loosen up. I need to check her over; let her breathe." Oscar's soft voice soothes. Shit, I didn't realize. I instantly retract my tight embrace.

"She's okay. She's in shock, though. Severe shock." Oscar stares at me pointedly.

"Shock at what?" Cal asks, fidgeting by his side. "What happened?"

"Did she say anything to you?" Oscar asks, watching me, his intense stare almost accusing.

"No, nothing. She just went to shower." I brush my thumb over her forehead. Her beautiful eyes looked straight through me, completely unaware of the surrounding turmoil.

"When will she wake up?" Bren asks as he sits down on the couch, his eyes still frozen on Angel.

"Could be a while," Oscar all but mutters as he turns and begins fiddling with his tablet.

"What are you doing?" Cal asks.

"She can't go to the hospital," I quickly snipe out.

Oscar sighs and drops his head, as if annoyed at my stupid question, before turning his gaze toward me. "I'm checking the cameras," he glances around the room with his eyes, informing me he's checking up on what went wrong.

"Don't go back too far," a jealous protective wave races through me at the thought of my brothers seeing my girl naked. Oscar nods as if understanding what I'm trying to tell him.

"Here," he points to the screen in my bedroom; my fists tightening at the thought that he can access my fucking bedroom with the goddamn cameras, my jaw tics in aggravation and I glare at him. Oscar ignores me and turns the screen as Cal crouches down to view it alongside Bren and me.

We watch as Angel moves to open the door before her whole body shakes, her face pales and her lips part as if she's willing them to speak. Her body drops to the floor like she's been shot. She clutches at her throat while struggling to hold her head up. My gut churns at the images of my girl, completely broken, trying to crawl along the carpet toward the closet, her fists tighten and each movement seems to be physically painful for her. My heart misses a beat at the soul-destroying sound of her sweet innocent voice choking while trying to recite that mother fucking prayer.

My shoulders tense, and my fists tighten. "She heard something." Cal's voice was low and barely audible.

Oscar nods in agreement. "Someone."

I shake my head, "It was just me and…" My body jolts, shock working its way down my body. I don't watch the tablet because I already know how the scene plays out in the living area. I was there. I was goddamn fucking there when just beyond the door, my girl was breaking down, crumbling to a broken form of herself. Just beyond the door.

"Don?" Bren questions.

All eyes dart toward Angel, then sympathetic eyes reach mine one by one, holding me in their vise-like clutches. I glance away from the intensity and peer down at my girl, "I don't… I don't understand." But I do. I do understand. I understand Don's voice shook my girl to a pulp. What I don't understand is why.

"We wait." Oscar motions toward Angel and takes a seat opposite me, watching and waiting for an explanation.

———

We sit in silence for over an hour. Oscar works away on his tablet while my eyes struggle to leave my girl's deflated body. Her lips moving once in a while, and I will them to release words I desperately need to hear. For true confirmation that she's okay.

She gasps and clutches her small fist against my shirt, wrapping it around her as if bringing herself closer to me. I sit her upright on my knee and take her chin between my fore-finger and thumb. "You with me, Angel?" I stare deep into her unsettled, distressed eyes. She swallows thickly, then ducks her head gently. "Good girl," I praise her, my words settling between us.

Cal hands me a bottle of water and I hold it to her lips. Slowly, she swallows the liquid down, before stilling and throwing her gaze round the room, around my brothers.

Her nails bite into my thigh through my joggers. Her chest heaving in panic, I stroke her spine gently, "Sshhh, it's okay, Angel. It's okay." She closes her eyes tightly, refusing to accept my words. My blood is boiling desperately to find out what the fuck is going on. What the fuck is happening?

"Angel, open your eyes and look at me," Oscar commands in a placid but no-nonsense tone, kneeling before her. Her eyes flare open. "You had a panic attack, and you suffer from PTSD. Is that right?" Angel dips her head slowly, agreeing

157

with Oscar's analysis. My hand draws circles lazily on her spine, my own spine rigid with anticipation, yearning for answers.

"His voice triggered you?" He asks but again also confirming.

Her eyes squeeze shut, and her body vibrates, her hands clutching into the material of my joggers. "Open your eyes, darlin'," I gently coax. She instantly responds, doing just as I ask. "Good girl."

Oscar licks his lips and sighs heavily. My heart thuds against my chest. Concerned by my own brother's actions, I grit my teeth, knowing whatever he's going to ask her is going to make her uncomfortable as fuck and potentially hurt her further. But also knowing that we need an answer. Oscar's eyes glance up at me, silently drilling into me for reassurance. I nod at him begrudgingly, knowing what needs to be done.

"He hurt you, didn't he?" My body jerks in shock. Fury races through me. What the hell did he just say? Who the fuck hurt her?

Angel nods, her lip quivering, and a small whimper escapes her chapped lips.

"Oscar." Bren's firm voice snaps me out of myself. My eyes catch onto Bren beside me, stiff as a board, veins popping at the side of his shaved head. Cal fidgets awkwardly in the chair opposite. His eyes focused purely on my girl.

Oscar ignores Bren and continues on gently, "Can you tell me what happened?"

Angel's chest begins to rise and fall rapidly. She glances at me desperately; soft whimpers escape her, her frantic eyes search my face for something, overrun with complete panic. "Shh, it's okay darlin', I got you." I stroke her spine and band my arm around her tightly; she nuzzles into my neck, her scent filling my nostrils.

"Angel…" Oscar's firm voice brings her attention back to him. "When did he hurt you?"

Her lips part, "Wh… when Finn left."

"Is that why you left? He hurt you?" Oscar quizzes before my mind can play catch up on what Angel just said.

Angel shakes her head, "Th… they took me away." Her vulnerable eyes meet mine as if her words explain everything. They explain fuck all. Annoyance clutching at my insides. "Someone hurt you?" I grasp her chin in my hand. She nods in agreement.

"Uncle Don hurt you? That's what you're saying?" Bren's voice booms through the room, causing Angel to jump.

"Back the fuck up!" I spit in his direction before glancing down at my girl for her to answer. She nods. A stuttered gasp escapes my throat as my body shakes, my heart lurching. He hurt her? My uncle Don hurt her?

Cal moves forward and sits beside Angel; he tucks a strand of hair gently behind her ear. I shove him away, my eyes alight with fury. Fuck him for touching my girl. "Get the fuck away from her!"

Cal ducks his head. "We need to know." The words were so quiet I barely hear them. "He's our uncle. We need to know," he repeats, clearly struggling too.

"Angel, who took you away?" Oscar coaxes.

Angel's hand goes to my dog tags. Clutching them in her hands, she swallows audibly. "They did. The men, they took me away."

Oscar's eyebrows knit together in confusion with her strange, riddled answers. "Who were they? Do you know who they were?" She shakes her head solemnly.

I meet Oscar's eyes, and he sighs, almost a sigh of defeat.

"Angel darlin', look at me." I grasp her chin in my palm. "You need to tell us everything." She shakes her head, her body vibrating on my own. Her hands pull up to tug her hair. "I can't. I can't!" I grab her wrists in annoyance. "Fuckin stop,

Angel. Listen to me. Listen," her eyes meet mine, unadulterated fear seeping through them; I can see the turmoil of the trauma. "I want to hear it. I need to know."

She shakes her head more vigorously, her voice pleading, "No. No, you don't, Finn. No, please don't."

"Angel, listen to me." I lick my lips. "I love you, darlin'; we need to do this so we can move on. You need to do this. Nothin' you say is going to stop me from lovin' you. Ya hear me? I'm yours and you're mine, I swear it." Her eyes soften and a tremor works through her body; goosebumps cover her skin.

Her voice is low. "I'm sorry." Her lips tremble and a lone tear escapes down her beautiful face. She closes her eyes and her body seems to give in with the acceptance I'm so desperate for. She opens her eyes with renewed confidence. Her eyes concentrating on the wall beside us.

CHAPTER 21

Angel

I stare at the wall, practically zoning out, concentrating on a small speck on the paintwork. I try to shut them out so I can explain. I swallow thickly, my throat clogging. "It was when you were away." I ignore them all and continue, "I came home from church and when I got inside, her pimp was in the room."

I play with Finn's dog tags, the weight feeling too heavy from my usual St. Christopher cross. I smile to myself, remembering Finn gifting it to me the day he left to join the Army. All his brothers had one, but Finn wore his all the time; I would play with it while I lay with my head on his chest, he gave it to me to look after, telling me we'd be together again soon and start our life together, it was going to be my lifeline. It is my lifeline, only not in the way he intended.

Finn's hand draws circles on my back, bringing me to the here and now, relaxing me slightly and giving me encouragement to continue. I take a deep breath. "I didn't realize it was him."

"Who?" Cal stares at me dumbly. The thought makes me chuckle.

"Your Uncle Don." I bite my lip at the shock and confusion running over his face before his eyes leave mine, no doubt looking over at his brothers.

I can see Oscar nodding out of the corner of my eye as if confirming my words. "He said my mom had sold me."

The words come out a lot more confident than I feel. Finn's spine straightens, his hands ball into fists, but I ignore his reaction and carry on. "He said I'd make him a fortune." I drop my head on a chuckle. "He was fucking wrong." I shake my head and laugh to myself, no doubt coming across as insane as I feel.

"What happened next?" Oscar asks as he subtly types on his tablet.

"I proved them wrong." I shake my head at the memories flashing before me.

"What does that mean, Angel?" Oscar asks, his eyes analyzing me expertly.

I swallow, my throat is scratchy and dry. Finn shifts slightly beneath me, his hand drawing circles on my back once again. I play with my fingers in my hands. "They had a doctor there, at the warehouse. He checked me." I close my eyes quickly, desperate to eradicate the sickening memory.

"A doctor?" Finn's voice is laced with venom. I nod.

"They were checking your virginity?" Oscar asks with a slight uncertainty in his tone. He gets it. He understands.

Finn stills beside me, freezing. I don't want to look at him. To see the pain in his eyes. I stare ahead at the wall and nod softly, "Yes."

I hear Bren suck in the air behind me, no doubt rigid and tight with anger.

I stare at the wall.

"I proved them wrong."

I can sense them all, feel the understanding of the weight of my words, layering the tension of the room. They know I was Finn's girl; they know I proved them wrong. I wasn't a virgin.

I wasn't going to earn him a fortune.

Oscar shuffles on the floor beside me, his voice is uneasy. "Then what happened, Angel?"

"I... I." I lick my lips, unable to get the words out.

And he's there, stroking my back again. "Shhh, darlin'. It's okay, you tell us. It's okay. I'm here. Finn's here."

My breath hitches. "I made him angry." I shake my head as the memories flick in front of my eyes like yesterday. Like every night when I close my eyes and see it, feel it.

"He was mad. So mad." I shake my head, the words tumbling from my mouth. "He pushed me against the table. He grabbed my hair." My hand flies up to my head, still feeling the sting of his grasp. "He hit me and hit me." I touch my lip, my cheek, my eyebrow.

My words come out like his, laced with rage and hate. "You whore, just like your Mom. I'm going to fuck you and sell you like the whore you are, you filthy little whore. You were meant to be pure; you were meant to earn me good money. Fucking whore!" My voice grows higher. Tighter, each word feeling like a knife cutting through my heart.

"Jesus." Finn sighs beside me, his hand shaking, struggling to maintain the swirling motion of comforting me.

I'm not sure if it's fury or shock, maybe both?

"I'll kill him." Bren grinds out, his words a promise.

Finn

I've never struggled so much to sit through such trauma and not give off any emotion. Not wanting Angel to know how goddamn hard it is to act unaffected by my girl's words.

She says them like she's playing the whole scene out again in front of her, and in a way, I guess she is. Guilt curdles inside me.

"Did he touch you?" Oscar's soft voice cuts into the tension-filled room. I wait, my heart missing a beat as I wait, almost praying for it not to be true.

She squeezes her eyes shut; her body shakes from her feet to her head. I suck in a sharp breath, already knowing the answer. A loud bang draws my eyes open as I sit, completely unaware I'd even closed them.

Bren throws himself back on the couch, palming his fist from the assault on my wall.

Angel's shoulders slacken. My hands tremble, struggling to continue to draw the circles on her spine that have helped her relax. I force myself to do it for her.

A sheen of sweat is beaded on her forehead.

My stomach knots and a ball of sickness forms, "He... he," I stutter my words out, nausea coating my throat, "he raped you?"

Angel whimpers and clamps her mouth shut; her hands find her throat.

"Did he hurt your throat, Angel?" Cal asks wide-eyed, his pupils blown in obvious discomfort. I realize now, that she's been leaving me clues, almost acting out the scene for me. She's been silently replaying over what's happened to her. I swallow down the bile. My vision blurry through a haze of tears and rage.

"Take his cock, whore, take him while I fuck you." She hisses and touches her chest as though something had hit her.

My eyes dart to Cal's, his own brow furrowed in confusion. "A chain." She explains, staring at the wall.

"Chain?" Oscar asks in confusion.

"The one he hit me with and put around my throat. I couldn't breathe." She touches her chest. "Couldn't swallow." She clutches her throat. "They were laughing at me." My palms ball into fists, a twitch rippling through my body, desperate to release the aggression. To make someone pay.

To make him pay.

"How many were there?" Oscar gives away no emotion as he asks the questions clinically.

"Three."

"Including Don?"

Angel nods.

"Do you know who the other two were?"

She gently shakes her head. "No. They had accents."

My interest peaks. I lick my lips to wet the dryness coating them. "What sort of accents, darlin'?"

Her eyes meet mine, unshed tears encompassing them. "The older one was Russian, I think." She touches her cheek. "He had a scar." She draws a finger down her cheek and my body vibrates with confirmation. Igor Dimitriev. "He had a gold tooth, too." She squeezes her eyes closed. "When he laughed, I saw it." I grind my teeth and try to surpass a growl.

"Dead man walking," Bren's firm, gruff voice adds, confirming he knows.

"What about the other?" Oscar asks. Ignoring our primal need to rip something apart. Someone.

"Mexican, I think. He was young," Angel swallows harshly, her eyes ducking down. "Reluctant."

My hands curl at her words. "Reluctant to do what, darlin?"

Her lips tremble. "Hurt me like that." She clutches my dog tags. "Like they did."

Her voice drops again. "You need to prove yourself, kid. Prove you've got what it takes to help run this empire. Now pull the bitch's leash and fuck her ass, hard. Make her scream like the whore she is." Acid bubbles up my throat. I close my eyes and try to control my breathing, to rein in my temper, to wash away the overwhelming urge to vomit.

"I get her pussy. You two can have her ass. Fuck her up. Isn't that right, little whore? Scream for Jesus, pray for your god to save you? For Finn to save you." She hisses and gurgles, clutching her throat with her mouth dropping open, "Pray, let me hear you pray." A small whimper escapes her, and I pull her into me, onto my chest, as I hold her sobbing, broken body. I hold her, rocking backward and forward with my girl. I watch as our tears mix, our chests rising and falling in unison.

Finally, understanding the meaning behind that god damn prayer. My jaw clenches painfully.

Angel lifts her head from my chest and stares almost emptily. "The... the chains." She holds up her wrists once again, trying to tell me something. I realize she's trying to tell me more; I swallow and nod at her wrists. "They put chains on your wrists?"

Angel nods, her voice low, weak, a whisper. "Yes, in the box."

The room is silent as we try to process her words.

"What box, Angel?" Oscar asks eagerly.

"The one in the warehouse." Her eyebrows knit together, deep in thought. "The crate."

"Darlin' I..." my face watches hers, unsure what she's trying to tell me.

She licks her lips, and her eyes become aggravated that I'm not understanding her. "The crate. They put me in a crate with chains."

"They were shipping you?" Bren asks, his voice deep and stern.

"Yes." She tugs on her wrists, so I take them in my hand and gently brush my fingers over them, effectively taking away the chains. She nods at me in approval. So fucking fucked up.

"The truck stopped, and I screamed and screamed for help. A man he got out of the truck and opened the crate. He didn't know." She shakes her head. "He didn't know. He gave me money. Told me to run, to never come back." Her eyes meet mine, determination shining through them.

I dip my head in understanding. She didn't leave me; she didn't have a choice. I pull her into me, holding her head in my hands, and kiss her lips, a gentle acknowledgment and gratitude. My girl didn't run.

She didn't leave me.

She didn't have a choice.

"Angel, do you know where they were shipping you?"

"No, but it differed from the other crates. It had a blue sticker on it."

I meet Oscar's eyes, his eyes alight with intrigue, and mine alight for vengeance.

CHAPTER 22

Finn

Angel's completely spent. Drained, emotionally and physically. I tuck her under a blanket on the couch, her eyes staring hollowly toward nothing. Again.

The room is eerily silent as we all sit dumbstruck. Our thoughts are racing but ultimately gaining nothing but pain.

I drop my head into my hands, my whole-body feeling like it's giving way. Without further warning, uncontrollable sobs rack through me, my heart broken at the core. I let her down.

I thought I was building us a dream when in reality, I created her worst nightmare.

"Finn. We've got you, man." Cal's hand brushes my shoulder protectively. I can barely acknowledge it. How did we not know? How could someone we love do this to us? To his own family?

"He'll pay Finn. Swear to fuck; he'll pay." Bren's sharp words break the silence like a knife cutting through the tenderness of succulent meat.

"The damage is already done. He already hurt her, Bren."

I glare at him through my swollen eyes. "He fucking brutal-ized her. She never hurt a fuckin soul, never." My voice cracks, but clear rage and intent seep through.

"I know." He nods solemnly. "I know."

Oscar's phone breaks us out of our trances. He turns toward Cal and rolls his eyes. "Reece."

Cal motions for him to answer it. Oscar's face glares coldly at the phone before putting it on speaker. "I'm in a meeting, Reece."

"Like fuck you are. Why the hell is Finn's apartment flashing on the security app?"

Oscar's eyebrows knit together but he doesn't raise his head from glaring at the phone sitting before him. "Explain." His voice was deep and curt.

"It came up on my app. There's been a security breach on Finn's cameras."

Oscar frantically begins typing away on his tablet. I glance at Cal, who gazes at Bren, and then back toward me.

"I don't understand. Nothing is showing on my screen. Security is activated." Oscar clips back.

Reece's voice is clear and confident, almost a replica of Oscar's. "Yeah, I realize that. That's why I'm calling." His tone laced with irritation. "My own system I use as a backup. Swear to fuck. Someone's fucking with the system they can see in the apartment, Oscar. What the fuck are they looking for?"

My heart goes wild as I stare back over my shoulder at Angel's sleeping form.

Oscar's deep voice penetrates the room. "Reece. Black-bird." He cuts the call. Cal's frantic eyes find mine. The last time our code word "Blackbird" was used, Lily and Reece had been kidnapped. We have a procedure in place that only close family knows about. Thankfully, Don's not one of them.

Angel's phone buzzes across the glass table. I move to pick it up, noticing Charlie's school name dancing on the screen. As if she has some sort of sixth sense, Angel stirs. "Darlin', the school is calling you." I hand her the phone.

"Put it on speaker!" Oscar virtually screams at Angel, making her jump. She's oblivious to the fact we're about to go on a lockdown. Cal paces up and down the room, tugging on his hair.

Angel's hand shakes as she answers the call. "Hello."

"Chelsea Danes?"

"Yes. That's me." Angels' eyes meet mine warily, and I nod at her in encouragement.

"Oh, thank goodness, Miss Danes. This is Ms. Catton, the principal at Derry Elementary school. I've just been informed that during an outdoor activity this morning, Charlie has gone missing. Now I'm sure this is all some prank gone wrong. We've informed the local sheriff's department and they are out searching." Angel's desperate face finds mine, her eyes searching mine for help, her mouth open wide. She holds the phone away from her white face, tears falling from her eyes silently. Her hands shake uncontrollably, much like my own.

"He knows," Oscar speaks low, almost to himself.

"He knows?" Angel's panicked eyes find mine as she repeats the question. "He knows?" I nod at her. "He knows about Charlie? He knows. Oh my god, he's got Charlie." She becomes hysterical, standing and tugging her hair; she drops the phone to the floor.

I jump up to comfort her. "Darlin', I don't think…"

"FINN!" I turn toward Oscar's deep voice, his eyes are cold and menacing. Each word was emphasized. "He. Knows." Panic bubbles up inside me.

"Angel. Is Don Charlie's father?" Oscar asks out of the blue. I glare at the insinuation. How the fuck dare… Oh fucking Jesus. Sickness roils inside me, almost bringing me to my knees. I scrub a hand through my hair. My princess is the product of rape? I'm going to kill the motherfucker.

Angel lets out a gut-wrenching wail. The sound reverberating in my stomach. She falls to the floor on all fours, gasping for air. Her fists clench. "He knows. He's taken my baby, please. Please help me."

I spin around on my heel, staring at my brothers desperately for someone to do something. Helplessness floods my veins.

Bren stands abruptly, causing my eyes to turn in his direction. "Finn, get Angel. Code Blackbird. Move. Now." His words are concise and commanding.

I don't think I act. I scoop Angel's fetal-like form into my arms. Cal and Bren pull out their guns as we make our way to the exit. Oscar types rapidly away on his tablet, standing between them both.

————

We've made our way over to Cal's old apartment. Our version of a safe house. It's situated above Oscar's own and therefore has more mod-cons and security than a prison itself.

We burst through the door. Lily throws herself in Cal's arms. "Are you okay? What the hell's happening?" Her eyes scan his body for evidence of injury.

"What the fuck's going down?" Con comes barreling through us in the doorway with the yapping bold shit he calls a dog hot on his heels. I've barely stepped over the threshold before the questions start.

He searches my face before his eyes fall on Angel's shell-shocked body. Her eyes staring emptily into nothingness. Con's eyes scrutinize the lax body I cling desperately to in my arms. His eyes bug out with awareness. "Holy fuck. Is that?" He splutters. I nod.

I push past him and make my way into one of the bedrooms. His footsteps follow me.

"Jesus, Finn. What the fuck's happened to her?" My footing wavers at the enormity of his words. Too much has happened to her.

"Con? Con. Who is that?" I hear Will traipsing behind Con, who's now following me into the bedroom. No doubt wanting her own answers.

His footfalls pause and his voice is a sympathetic whisper. "It's Angel, baby."

"Angel? Angel?"

I squeeze my eyes shut at the excitement in Will's voice.

Gently, I place Angel down on the comforter just as Will comes into the room. Her wavy brown hair flies loosely around her face, making her look younger than she really is. Her eyes land on Angel, her body jolts slightly, and an awareness seeps in. "Finn..." her voice trembles. "What happened to her?" I squeeze my eyes closed, not wanting to admit the truth and deal with the fallout. The severity.

"Finn. Are you okay?" Con's hand squeezes my shoulder and I open my eyes, not realizing I'd closed them.

I shake my head from side to side. "No. No man, I'm not." I turn and meet my little brother's bright blue eyes. His eyebrows narrow in confusion before he pulls me in for a very unexpected but grateful hug.

"We've got you, brother." His calm voice soothes me as he holds me tight.

"She's... she's in shock, right?" Will's voice draws me away from Con. Her eyes search mine in question where she's sitting on the bed beside Angel, stroking her hair gently from her face.

"Yeah. She's had a traumatic day." I almost choke on the irony. Traumatic day? More like traumatic life. She's been through fucking hell.

Will moves to kneel beside Angel softly, talking to her. Tears drip down Will's face as she tells her how much she's missed her and how she promises she's safe now.

I only hope what she's telling her is the truth, and we can deliver on her promises.

CHAPTER 23

Finn

We're gathered in the den. A room Oscar has dedicated to the security system and his technology. Bren stands like a guard at the door, his muscular body filling the frame. Con has his head in his hands after Cal gave him a rundown of what has happened. Oscar types manically away on his keyboard and I stare into space, struggling to stay with the here and now.

"What's the plan?" Bren's deep voice cuts into the silent room.

My head shoots up toward Oscar. He turns on his chair, his attention now fully on us. "We don't know who is compromised." He grimaces, implying we don't know who in our security team we can trust.

"We do this ourselves," Bren adds. I nod in approval.

"You think he'll hurt her? Does he know he's her…"

I cut Con off, "He's not her fucking father, Con! They're mine; they both are. And I'm the one that kills him. You hear me?" My eyes scan around my brothers as they all nod in agreement.

"Okay, so his trackers aren't on. So, he's expecting us. By

now, I'm sure he knows we know. But we need to be aware he hasn't done this alone." Oscar grimaces.

"Perhaps we should split up into teams? Someone needs to deal with Igor Dimitriev." Cal suggests.

My heart thunders in my chest at the mention of the sick prick's name. I shoot up from my chair. "Me, he's mine."

Oscar puts his hand up to calm me. He shakes his head. "We don't split up. We do this together; I need you to get information from him before you finish him, Finn." His eyes drill into mine with severity as I take my seat again, "Information is key." Oscar emphasizes, his eyes don't leave my own. I duck my head knowingly.

Banging at the door breaks the tension. "Open up motherfuckers. Let me fucking in." Jesus, it's Reece. I glance at Cal. He's pinching his nose, and then his hands brush wildly through his hair before he looks up at the ceiling. The poor guy has his hands full.

"Fuck off!" Bren bellows back.

"Let me the fuck in!" Reece roars.

Oscar waves at Bren, motioning for him to open the door. Bren visibly sighs and turns with a roll of his eyes to unlock the door.

Reece barrels into the room, his eyes wildly searching us all for answers. He straightens his shoulders and stands in front of Oscar. "Okay, what shall I do?"

"Look after the women and kids." Cal clips out with a deadpan face.

Reece spins around to face his father, venom oozing from his eyes. "You jackass motherfucker. I bring more to this team than you." Reece's shoulders broaden as he points at his father, "I can tell you where Igor Dimitriev is hiding." He gloats with a smirk.

All our spines straighten at the mention of his name.

"Reece, I need that information now." Oscar's nononsense voice cuts in before softening, "We need you here

Reece, to protect our families. I need you to maintain a security barrier around the apartment. Nobody comes in or out of the building or security system."

Reece nods in understanding, taking a moment before replying. "Of course. I'm going to set up a trip wire on this floor, you know, just in case." he shrugs.

Cal chokes in a panic. "Trip wire?"

Reece faces Cal, "Yeah, you know. The bad guys come... boom, boom... no legs left, motherfucker. Blow the cunts off." Reece makes hand gestures about a bomb going off.

Cal's eyes nearly leave their sockets. If I wasn't so on edge, I'd be pissing in my boxers. "Jesus." Cal huffs and glares at us in despair.

"No trip wire, Reece. You maintain a safe environment with the technology provided to you."

Reece's shoulder sags. "You guys are no fun sometimes." He tugs on his hair in frustration. "Fine. No fucking trip wire, but I get a weapon." I glance up at Bren, whose lip is curved in amusement.

———

We decided it was kinder to Angel to sedate her, the plan being by the time she wakes, princess will be back in her mama's arms, and Angel won't have endured any more trauma than she has already.

After getting the relevant information from Reece, we head over to a small warehouse on the outskirts of town. Cal drives with me sitting shotgun and Oscar orchestrating from the back what we're about to do.

Bren is driving his G-Wagon upfront with Con; they're going to blow open the gates with a rocket launcher, gaining us entry, then we split into two teams and search the warehouse for Igor, taking out each and every fucker in our way.

Reece has been keeping tabs on our Russian rivals for a

while now, which is both a good thing and also a little worrying. Cal seriously needs to get a handle on his kid. He's a loose cannon.

As if hearing my thoughts, Cal speaks almost to himself. "Reece is fucking obsessed with these Russian bastards."

Oscar leans forward between the seats. "I think you'll find it's Boris. Igor's nephew he's obsessed with."

Cal's eyebrows shoot up. Did Oscar just imply Reece has a thing for this Boris kid? As if sensing Cal's thoughts, "Let me clarify, Reece is obsessed with a girl that Boris has his eye on."

Cal relaxes slightly before Oscar's words sink in. The moment they do, his spine straightens again. "What fucking girl? How the hell do you know this?"

Oscar waves his hand in Cal's direction as if to shush him. "We're two minutes out."

I sit up in my seat straighter and keep my eyes on the G-Wagon ahead, now speeding toward a metal gate. As if in slow motion, Con's window goes down and out comes the launcher.

"NOW!" Oscar barks from behind me.

The noise penetrates the air with a deafening whistle. The G-Wagon disappears into the smoke ahead. Our own car shakes from the aftermath but continues to drive on, following through the thick dust and debris. "Make an immediate left after the target," Oscar instructs Cal.

The car swerves to the left, and without further instruction, we all jump out of the vehicle and have our weapons drawn. "Clear." Bren's voice booms from the small warehouse ahead.

"Cal, go cover Con, around the back of the warehouse." Oscar stands straight with a sneer, glancing down at his normally impeccably polished shoes, now covered in dust and dirt. I watch his face as he seems lost in thought. For the first time, I recognize my brother is counting in his head. How often does he do this? Is this one of his coping mechanisms?

A whistle breaks my stare and causes Oscar's head to flick up. Bren waves us over. Scanning the area, I run over toward Bren with my handgun in position. Oscar's footsteps follow behind.

"Con took two outback. We think he's confined inside." Bren informs us.

"Good, we waste no time in case he's instructed backup; let's go." Oscar motions toward the door.

Bren kicks in the door with ease. The metal door bounces off the wall behind it.

Stepping into the warehouse, my eyes adjust to movement in the bottom right corner. I fire my gun without hesitation. Aiming it at the victim's legs, to maim, not to kill, just in case it's Igor. The body drops to the floor with a groan.

Bren takes the right-hand side, and Oscar follows me. "Con and Cal are in the building, two more guards down." He whispers.

A shadow rushes toward us and Bren ducks down before gripping the shadow at the waist and throwing him over his head. The guy drops to the floor with a thud and groan, and before Bren gets a chance to act, I swoop down. Withdrawing my knife, I plunge my blade into the side of his neck, taking pleasure in the life leaving his eyes.

We make our way over to the body that's dragging himself toward a weapon. His hand reaches out, desperately trying to grab his gun. I kick it away just as the fucker turns over. His ugly fucking scarred face brings both rage and joy.

The fucker's eyes meet mine before he chuckles.

"Ready to hear my secrets?" he taunts.

CHAPTER 24

Finn

"Ready to hear my secrets?" Igor's taunting words play in my head on repeat as Bren and Con drag his reluctant solid body toward a chair, his legs flay in every direction, attempting to delay the inevitable. I stare down at the Russian monster, the man that had helped brutalize my girl in the most horrific of ways. Bile rises in my throat, imagining Angel's terrified form staring into his marred face.

As Con uses zip ties to secure his arms and legs, I absently register Oscar explain that he's tapping into the poor security system to keep tabs on any backup that may or may not arrive.

All the while, I stare down at the man that helped tear my world apart, my eyes unable to leave him.

A hand touches my shoulder, causing me to flinch. "Are you ready for this?" I turn slightly, looking into Cal's concerned eyes. Is he worried about the secrets Igor's about to give or the horrors I'm about to hear?

He needn't worry about either of those things because when we leave here today, the torture Igor will endure will help ease the immense guilt I feel for Angel's torment. He'll pay alright, pay in flesh and blood.

My fists tighten and my teeth clench so hard my jaw aches; every cell on my body is running high on adrenaline, alert and ready to dispel carnage on his vile body.

Con and Bren move away from Igor. His mocking eyes meet mine. I scan him over, shaved head and scarred face. He licks his lips in jest before giving me a smirk. His teeth shine brightly, gold shimmering from one at the side. My mind recalls Angel's recollection. Yeah, the tooth is going to go. My eyes trace down his muscular form. He's in a crisp, fitted suit, his wrists strapped to the chair. His trouser leg stretched tightly over his thighs; the gunshot wound visibly oozing blood. Igor tests the restraints but cannot move himself because of his ankles being so tightly secured to each chair leg.

"When was your last contact with Don?" Oscar moves forward to analyze Igor's response. His firm voice cuts through the air.

Igor licks his lips as if contemplating his answer, then shakes his head and ignores Oscar's question. Stupid man, game fucking on.

I bend down, tug up my jeans, and unstrap the knife holster attached to my leg. Con throws a rucksack at my feet with a wink, and I know right now my brother has come prepared for me to complete my notorious Finn-finishing. A feeling of comfort and familiarity encompasses me as I open the bag.

I stand up slowly and give Igor my full attention. The grip on the hammer in my hands tightens with excitement as I watch his pupils dilate with fear. "Do you know what they call me?" I ask as I take a step toward him.

"A fucking psychopath?" He quips, still trying to make light of his shitty situation.

I feign a chuckle. "They nicknamed my skill set Finn-finishing." I lick my lips when he straightens his face, blood draining from it.

"Nails!" I demand to Con. He retrieves the bag of nails from the rucksack, handing them to me with a smirk.

"Fuck!" Igor mumbles as he tests the restraints again.

"Get rid of his clothes." I bark at Bren, making him jump into action, moving forward with an Army knife. He grips Igor by the neck and begins cutting off his clothes. Igor throws his head back, but Bren anticipates the movement and chuckles at his lame attempt to headbutt him. Igor seethes in temper and spits at Bren. Bren's spine straightens, and he releases Igor. Sneering down at him, he calmly wipes the spittle from his face using his arm, his glare menacing. He rears his arm back and delivers a jaw-crushing blow to Igor's face, the sound of the impact splitting through the room. The chair wobbles with the force. Bren spits back at Igor before stepping back and motioning toward me with his hand and a snide smile. "He's all yours, brother."

Moving into position, I grab a nail, place it against Igor's arm and lift my hammer, enjoying the thrill of his agony when the nail rips through his skin and hits the bone.

"Jesus. Fuck, man." A screech and repeated expletives leave his mouth as I continue lining up the nails one by one and hammering them into his arm, the delicious sound of his screeching leaving his filthy mouth. "Fuck. Motherfucker, Motherfucker." His Russian accent thickening with each insertion.

His arm oozes blood, the limb resembling a mockup of the horror movie 'Hellraiser.'

Spittle trails down his mouth. "Okay, shit, okay. I'll answer your questions." Desperation laces his pleading words.

I hammer in another for good measure as Igor attempts to thrash about away from me, but that only serves to bring him more pain. The flesh on his arm pushing tightly against his body's natural reaction to fight causes more rips in his flesh.

Oscar moves into my line of sight. "When was your last communication with Don?"

Igor pants, his lip now bleeding from biting down on it. "Two days ago. He told me nothing. I swear he never mentioned you guys were coming." His chest rises and falls as the words drip from his torn lips; dribble flows from his mouth, no doubt because of the fist Bren administered. "He never gave me a heads up. Left me here like a lamb to the slaughter." He tilts his head in my direction.

"You think he left him here as a distraction?" Cal asks Oscar, stepping forward, rubbing a forefinger over his lips in thought.

"No. I think he panicked and fled."

"With my fucking kid!" I snap at Oscar.

Igor's eyes fly open. "A kid? Honestly, I don't know anything about a kid man. I swear. I don't hurt kids." Is he seriously trying to redeem himself somehow?

"No, you just rape innocent young girls, right?" Bren snipes from beside me. My spine bolts upright at the statement.

Igor's eyes meet my own. I can feel the darkness ooze out of mine and seep into his body. He shudders slightly with the same realization before drawing in a sharp, deep breath. "I didn't know she was your girl, Finn, not until she said your name. He never told us." His thick Russian accent seeps through his words. He shakes his head. Is he trying to convince himself or me?

"Didn't know she was my girl until she begged for mercy, you mean?" I drop the hammer; the clanging noise vibrates around us, causing Igor to flinch. Retrieving an alternative knife from my holster, I smile at him manically. "Well, let me make one thing clear, motherfucker. You will be begging for mercy; my eyes will be the last thing you see when I scoop them out and crush them one by one." I slice into his chest. Deep. Deep enough to make the scumbag howl, his skin flaps open. He screams like a bitch, the sound only fueling my need to satisfy my internal craving. His blood flows down his body like a river.

He stumbles over his words. "I'm… ss… sorry. Fuck. I'll… I'll tell you everything." His blood-coated spit drizzles down his chin.

I move to his thighs, taking pleasure in his discomfort. My eyes lock on his already open wound. I dig my knife into the bullet holes and dig around. All the while, Igor shakes, and tussles. Retrieving the bullet, I lean over his battered body and pry his injured jaw open. Con steps forward to take hold of the top of his head and upper jaw. I smile at him, his eye bugging out in fear as I drop the bullet down his throat. I take sick satisfaction at the choking sounds. "Swallow, mother-fucker; otherwise you'll be swallowing your cock next." His eyes bulge at the threat, his breath quickens in panic. I give Con a nod and he releases his jaw at the same time as me. We watch Igor move his head forward and swallow the bullet.

CHAPTER 25

Finn

Igor loses his toe and fingernails thanks to my little brother, Con. The cocky little shit takes after me for having a thirst for blood. I take pleasure in pulling out his teeth, the offending gold one going first. His mouth was a completely mangled mess.

"Is your brother involved in this?" Oscar asks.

Igor moves his head from side to side slowly. "No, I didn't want him involved, not with the shit Don is into." My attention is piqued. He didn't want his younger brother involved in this sick setup, but he thought to involve innocents.

"We want to know of any places Don might be hiding from us," Cal asks, stepping forward from the shadows.

Igor throws his battered head back and attempts to laugh, blood now trailing uncontrollably down his chest. "There's too many to mention."

Oscar twitches slightly, obviously not happy with this latest development. Oscar is normally so in tune with everyone that this will have shaken him. The fact that not only is our uncle a monster, but he's managed to outwit and deceive us all. We trusted him; no reason to ever doubt his intentions. Never.

My veins pulsate on my forehead with tension. This playing around shit is getting us nowhere. We need some information and fast so I can get princess back with her mama before she wakes. An unsettling feeling of uncertainty curdles in my stomach, but I refuse to take notice.

"Cut off his cock." I bark at Con.

"Oh, fuck no. Wait, wait." His words come out rapidly. "I know nothing about the kid. Didn't even know one existed."

"How did you come about working with Don, and what exactly were you doing?" Oscar's straight, no-nonsense voice perforates the growing tension.

"I worked with him for years." He tries to lick his lips, but his face is so swollen you can barely see his tongue, his speech slurring. "He took me under his wing, and he initiated me into his circle. We kept our distance for pretenses' sake." Igor's chest moves up and down rapidly, the wounds now taking effect. "Don fed us information about your shipments, and we acted on it. He took a cut on the shipments." He sluggishly attempts to lift a shoulder but flinches in pain when he isn't able to.

"Initiated?" Oscar muses, staring at him with a deadpan face.

Igor darts his eyes away from me, ducking his head slightly. "Yeah, hurting women."

"Rape?" Oscar quizzes.

My shoulders tighten and my heart races against my chest in rage. I struggle to hold in the need to hurt him but realize I have to hold back for Oscar to get his answers. Then the fucker can pay. Cal moves into my line of sight, no doubt ready to stop me from lunging at the scum in question.

Igor ducks his head, "Yeah, rape."

"You sick motherfucker!" Bren bellows and rushes toward

him. He's like a fucking bull; grabs the hammer off the floor and smashes it against Igor's face with a resounding clunk.

Both me and Cal restrain Bren, bringing him away at a safe distance. "He's mine brother," I whisper reassuringly into his ear. Slowly, Bren's breathing calms down and he relaxes against me.

Moving back toward Igor. Oscar gives him no time to pull himself together. "What were his plans for Angel?" I stiffen at the mention of my girl's name.

Igor's head hangs. He tries to lift his heavy head, but to no avail. "His plans!" Oscar screams at him.

"Sell… sell her." Igor struggles to part with the words, his body fighting consciousness.

"To who?"

"At the compound." His head rocks backward. "Sell the girls." He slinks forward again, "Make more on virgins." The sick fucks.

"Human trafficking?" "Skin trade?" Oscar asks, his stone face giving off nothing. Unlike our own, disgust oozing from our pores.

Igor tries to nod, his words coming out faint. "Yeah."

"What about children?" A wave of sickness rushes over me. Both Con and Cal stand taller and move forward. *Please, god, no.* Both of them are fathers, their concern obvious. Both with kids that have been around our fucking uncle. My heart hammers painfully.

"Children?" Oscar quizzes louder when Igor doesn't respond.

One word. One word that destroys me inside and out. "Yeah."

"Motherfucker!" I scream as the dark beast inside consumes me. I race toward him with my knife. Bren pulls Oscar away just in time as I reap havoc on the piece of shit. His wails drive me on. I feel nothing as I skin the filthy fucking scum alive. I don't even feel satisfaction. How the hell can you ever get satisfaction from something like him? A monster.

I slaughter him with ease.

CHAPTER 26

F inn

As I finish cleaning myself up, I roughly scrub my hands in the sink in Igor's office. The blood swirling around as it goes down the drain doesn't give me the satisfaction I had hoped for. We need answers. I need princess back. I watch my brothers in the mirror above the sink.

The office is silent but for Cal, who's frantically searching through paperwork, looking for clues to give us some idea where the prick is holed up. Oscar taps away manically on his tablet, frustration now showing on the crease of his brow. Con sits in Igor's chair with his feet up on the desk, his face blank, staring into space, no doubt lost in his own mind, similar to my own. At least his family is safe. I brush off the thought, feeling annoyed at myself for even feeling the slightest bit of envy toward my brother.

I sigh in defeat as my mind wonders... he mentioned a fucking compound. Just how big is this skin trade of theirs? Repulsion coils inside me. And children? What the fuck? This was the same man we grew up with, loved to be around; he took us camping as kids, for god's sake.

The sound of a phone echoes around the office. Bren

grumbles in annoyance and pulls it from his trouser pocket. "It's Sam." He stares down at the phone before glancing up at Oscar.

Sam is on one of Don's security teams. We've used him ourselves, another one we've had around our family. I grimace at the thought. Is he involved? How many that we don't know of? Scrubbing a hand through my already wild hair, I turn to face them.

"Put it on speaker." Oscar's sharp tone demands.

Bren nods in confirmation before answering gruffly, "Yeah."

Sam's voice shakes, making my back straighten at the urgency behind it. "Bren, sir. I... I. Your uncle. I'm not doing anything to a kid, man. He has a girl, sir. Shit, he has a kid."

My chest rises and falls in panic. "Where the fuck is he?" I scream, lurching toward the phone in Bren's hand, desperate for answers. Cal moves toward me, attempting to give me comfort. Oscar motions with his hand for me to shut up. Well, fuck him. It isn't his kid he's got.

"Where are you, Sam? Are you with Don?" Bren asks, his voice deep and direct.

"No, sir. I'm outside," his voice quietens as if not to be overheard. "I don't know where we are. Some woods somewhere. He has her back at the cabin. Sir, I'm meant to be on watch. I'm not hurting a kid. I'm not doing shit like that." His voice rises again in panic.

"Sam, it's Cal here. Calm down, kid; you did good calling us. Is the girl okay?" Cal's diplomatic voice seems to ease Sam.

My chest rises rapidly at Cal's words. I squeeze my eyes shut. Please be okay, sweetheart.

"Sir, she was injected with something. She's sleeping in a bedroom. But I overheard Don order a chopper. I think he's leaving with the little girl."

I all but gasp. My throat tightens, clogged with desperate emotion.

"Fuck!" Bren's fists tighten beside him in anger too.

A fucking chopper? He's planning on running and taking her. Please, god no. My frantic eyes meet Cal's; pleading hopelessly into his. He shakes his head at me, in tune with my thoughts. Telling me he won't let that happen, we won't let that happen.

"How long do we have?" Oscar asks.

"Two hours, sir." My shoulders tighten at the time constraint.

"How many men does he have?" Oscar leads with a reassuring ease. All the while, no doubt constructing a plan.

"Twelve, sir. He's ordered more, too."

Oscar pinches the bridge of his nose. "I want you to protect the girl with your life, Sam. Keep a safe distance, but when the time comes, you guard her, do not raise suspicion. If she's being kept alone, leave her that way. When we arrive, you protect her, do you understand me?" Oscar's no-nonsense voice reverberates through the room.

"Yes, sir," Sam responds, sounding more confident with the instruction than the panicked voice from earlier.

"Good. Continue with the instructions Don has given you until the time comes."

"Yes, sir." Oscar nods and ends the call.

My muscles ache from the tension.

"He's at the cabin," Cal speaks softly, almost to himself.

The cabin where Don used to take us as kids. Every fucking summer, he'd take us. We would look forward to it, a chance to be ourselves and away from the demands our father set on us. It's secluded and not a great deal of security, which is probably why he chose to hide out there. He'd have assumed we would think he'd go somewhere with all the security enhancements, not somewhere with little. "At least we know the area." Oscar muses back while tapping away.

"Like the back of our fucking hands," Bren confirms almost with glee.

"He'll land the chopper down by the lake. It's the safest place." Con nods to himself.

"I got Don." I stare at my brothers one at a time, each meeting my eyes with a subtle nod in return

I bounce on the balls of my feet, eager to get moving, the anxiety rippling through my veins, blood pumping with adrenaline. Now we know where the fucker is hiding out.

We spend the next twenty minutes discussing a plan.

A plan to rid the world of another monster.

CHAPTER 27

F inn

We traveled as teams in separate vehicles. Cal and Bren in the G-Wagon are going in from the North, me and Con going in from the West toward the cabin, and Oscar will stay east to maintain a visual for us all.

It's taken us nearly an hour to get here. Bren and Cal are going to take out the men that are no doubt hiding out in the woods; then Cal is going to wait for the chopper to arrive. Luckily, our vehicles have an arsenal of explosives that will do the trick. Bren will then make his way toward the cabin to provide backup.

Oscar will be our eyes and ears, providing us with audio support, making it so that we will be able to communicate with one another via our earpieces.

He's already logged in to the cameras on the outside of the cabin, so we know exactly where the fuckers are located. Unfortunately, inside the cabin, the cameras had been disabled, so we literally don't know what we're walking in on.

Oscar will also be setting up a series of explosive traps along the roads into the grounds using military claymore mines detonated on a motion sensor to cut off any fuckers that think they can provide the sick fuck with support.

Con is going to climb up onto the roof once the sniper has been taken down and survey the internal setup, hopefully gaining access via a window. The target is to locate princess and get her the hell out unharmed. My throat goes dry at the thought of her being hurt. I scrub my hand through my hair in frustration with trepidation.

"Finn, are you ready for this?" Oscar asks from the backseat without raising his head from his tablet.

I swallow thickly and straighten my shoulders, meaning every word. "Born ready, brother."

Con holds his fist out for me to bump. His eyes briefly leave the road and catching on to mine; a confident smirk leaves his lips.

Let's do this shit.

————

We leave Oscar on the outskirts of the track at the Eastern point.

Con steers the car off the road and we both jump out in unison, making our way to the back of the vehicle.

Con opens the trunk and scans his finger alongside a small screen on the inside of the SUV. A beeping noise confirms his fingerprint identity, and the inside of the trunk opens out, giving access to an array of weapons in the hidden compartment. I pull out a Kevlar vest for both me and Con, throwing one at him. Con chuckles and starts to strap a legion of firearms and grenades onto his body. The adrenaline bounces off my brother and onto me, causing excitement to suddenly race through my veins at the familiarity of the weapons at my disposal. Following Con, I load myself up with weapons.

I strap the last knife to the inside of my leg and inhale the fresh air, scanning my eyes around the area.

I'm coming, princess.

Con checks his watch, and just on cue, Oscar speaks to us via the earpiece, "Bren and Cal in position. Ready?"

"Ready," Con confirms.

"Ready," I repeat eagerly.

Me and Con take off with a nod at one another. As agreed, we work our way through the woods, both heading in slightly different directions, me behind Con to cover his back. Both with Glocks in hand and an arsenal of weapons hidden on our bodies.

A shadow crosses over the trees and I speak into my microphone, "Down." No sooner has Con ducked down I pop off two bullets into the head of one of the guards. Con glances back at me with a smirk. My eyes scan the edge of the woods, my ears listening out for sounds of footfalls. "Clear," I confirm. Con takes off with me on his trail, darting from tree to tree for cover.

The whistling of the leaves above us and the cracking of branches at our feet would give anyone a paranoid edge, but the sheer adrenaline running through me blocks out any threat and welcomes the fight with open arms. Do your worst motherfuckers.

We both reach the edge of the tree line. Ducking low, we wait for Oscar to instruct us to move on. My eyes scan the cabin and note three men on the roof, two covered by camouflage that would normally be naked to the visible eye, but my training has provided me with an insight.

Oscar's voice speaks through my earpiece. "All in position, Bren and Cal have cleared the ground. Chopper ETA five minutes. Backup arriving in two minutes, we move on signal, three on the roof. Heat cam picked up four more inside."

My heart rate picks up as I stare at the men on the roof with intensity, my eyes scrutinizing the scene. Don is going to know we're coming, he probably knows we're here already. My hand shakes slightly, completely unlike me, but I can't get the thought of princess out of my head and what that sick bastard is capable of, the enormity of the situation taking its toll. I shove the thought down inside and close my eyes to regain composure.

"Thirty seconds."

I swallow thickly.

A series of booms erupt from behind us, the road toward the cabin ambushed by Oscar's mines. This is the signal. My feet take off before registering the noise fully. The crunching of gravel tells me Con is also heading toward the cabin. I aim my Glock at the roof and fire off a succession of bullets. "One target down," Oscar confirms.

Shit, I needed to get at least two to give Con a chance on the roof. "Forward." Oscar barks, no doubt knowing what I'm thinking. My feet hit the steps with indecisiveness. "Clear." Oscar reacts to my pausing. "Body left of the door." His abrupt voice leaves no sign of indecisiveness.

I tuck my Glock behind my back and pull out my knife. Kicking the door open, it ricochets off the wall. I waste no time ducking low, expecting the blow to come.

I slice into the guard's gut, causing him to stumble and wail. Swiftly standing, I grip my arm around his neck and slit his throat. His heavy body falls against me. I release it with a thud to the ground.

I can hear a fight breaking out on the roof and feel an overwhelming need to support my brother, but right now, I've more important things to do.

Before I can think, Don rushes me, tackling his body low into my gut. We stumble over the couch and fall to the ground, the force of him knocking the wind from me. My head bounces off the solid wooden floor with a crack, causing me to grimace. "Fuck." That hurt.

There's no doubt that Don is more solid and heavier than me, but I have age and stealth on my side. He rears his head up and hits me hard in the face with his forehead, stunning me for a moment. He grips my wrists and pries the knife from my hand, causing it to fall to the floor. His full, heavy body straddles me, a wicked gleam and smile on his face knowing he's got the upper hand.

Why have I never seen the venom and evil oozing from him before? The thought startles me. My chest aches at the realization. Why has my vision been so clouded?

"You're going to die here today, Finnley, just like your brothers." He gloats.

My spine straightens at his threat. "Not today, motherfucker."

I wrap my legs around him and throw myself up and over, taking the upper hand and now straddling him. I grab the knife, turning it and gripping it tightly. I plunge it into his stomach, his gasp filling me with ecstasy while continuously bashing his thick head against the ground to keep momentum.

A succession of popping noises and sharp pain have me stumbling over Don, my mouth dropping open in shock; my heart beats rapidly as my mind registers, that I've been shot multiple times.

Don pushes me off him and I easily fall to the side, my mind almost blank. His solid body grapples to stand. "Get the girl." His deep voice cuts through the fog in my mind. I hear a scuffle and yells, shots fired. Jesus, my head hurts and there's a pain in my shoulder, and stomach too.

I crawl toward my weapon, but Don's boot stomps down hard on my hand. Fuck, that hurt. I swallow at the sensation of my left hand being crushed beneath his boot.

Don looms above me. "Think you could take what was mine, Finn? You think I don't know she's mine?"

I glare up at him, his dark eyes full of hate, his face red and deranged. "She's not yours, you sick fuck." I spit the words back at him.

He sneers, his bloody teeth on display, "You think you can

overpower me? My empire? Your brother knew better than that. Look where he ended up." A shiver rushes up my spine.

My body jolts at his words, unsure of the meaning behind them. Surely he doesn't mean?

He throws his bloody head back on a laugh. "Didn't you know? Didn't you get that far in your quest for answers? Keenan stumbled across me one night, making adjustments to the crates." Sickness overwhelms me, and I squeeze my eyes closed at the pain of his words. He continues on, "Didn't have many choices but to feckin kill him, did I? Inquisitive little bastard." I stare into his eyes. He hurt Keenan? Killed him? How the fuck could he do that to him? To us? Da and ma? Who the fuck is he? His voice wanders, almost sounding detached from him, "They took what was mine once. I won't let them do that again." I barely hear his words as he lifts his hand, and I find myself staring down at the barrel of a gun.

An almighty crash comes from behind him. Bren has virtually skyrocketed himself into the air and pounced onto Don, the full weight of them both hitting the floor. Bren delivers blow after blow to Don's face. I struggle to my feet, giving Bren time to pause and assess the damage. Don's pulverized body barely inhales air. "You good?" Bren's sharp, concerned eyes meet mine from over his shoulder. I hold my left arm over my stomach, my shoulder sagging on its own accord. It's damaged badly, but I don't care. Don lets out a faint laugh; mine and Bren's eyes shoot toward him, his stomach bleeding openly from his shirt; if he didn't have head injuries, he'd die from that wound alone. "You think you won?" My eyes narrow. What the fuck is he talking about? Is this a game to him? Bren's shoulders tighten at the prick's voice. His voice low and sinister, with a taunting edge to it. "Tell your Ma I know. Tell her I have a surprise for her." He chuckles to himself before taking his last breath with a smile on his sick face.

Footsteps behind me make me spin on my heels. Con

walks through the entryway with a limp arm, but it's what's in his other arm that has my heart racing, my princess. I gasp as a flood of emotions overwhelms me. My feet move to my girl, and my shaking hand trails down her golden locks. I bury my head in her hair, my body vibrating with relief. "She's good, brother. Sleeping." I nod, a tear-filled choke leaving my throat.

Sam walks through the same doorway with blood seeping from his chest. My glazed eyes meet his. "You good?"

His startled eyes widen in shock as though what I'm asking is absurd. "No, I'm not fucking good. Con shot me." He waves his hand in Con's direction accusingly.

I draw my head back to look at my younger brother. He throws his head back, laughing. "Yeah, sorry about that. I didn't register you were a good guy." His eyes glimmer in jest.

"Fucking dumb shit." Bren chuckles.

"Clear." Oscar startles us all in one. Jesus, the dude needs to learn when to not kill a moment. I shake my head at the thought. My body is buzzing with a high of happiness.

CHAPTER 28

Finn

After settling Charlie down next to Angel, Oscar had our family doctor, Mr. Yates, waiting at the apartment to fix Con and me up. He's an old fucker, but the doc is paid well to keep his mouth shut, and Da says he's been in the family for years. Con has taken a bullet to his arm, whereas I'd taken three to my torso. Thankfully, the Kevlar vest saved me from causing a serious injury. Now I'm just bruised. The bullet in my shoulder was dug out and replaced with stitches. It hurt like a bitch, but I've had worse. I clearly have a broken hand. The fucking prick crushed multiple bones. Oh, and my nose is crooked as fuck. If the prick wasn't dead already, I'd have cut off his cock and fed it to him with sick satisfaction. The thought alone annoys the fuck out of me; he got off too light. Way too light. Cal has a few random cuts, and Bren is completely untouched, like the fucking incredible hulk.

We're gathered round in the Den going over the events of the day when all I really want to do is lay with my girls, have their scent on me. Hold them, knowing nobody has taken them from me and never will again.

"What do we know?" Bren asks.

"I've sent a team in to clear the bodies. The chopper is dust. I'm going to work my way through Don's computers, figure out what the hell he's been into all these years." Oscar shakes his head from side to side in disgust, a sneer on his lips.

"You think Da knew?" Con asks.

Cal hits him around the back of his head. "Of course, he didn't know. You stupid fuck. He might be a prick, but he's not a fucking monster." Con shrugs his shoulders with indifference as if the two are the same.

Sighing, I decide to let my brothers in on the bombshell Don had dropped on me, "Don said he was responsible for Keenan." Nausea swirls in my stomach.

Con jumps up from his chair. "What?" Shock and betrayal marring his face, the anguish playing out on his features. He was the one to find Keenan dead, and he's never forgiven himself for being the one to send him into the warehouse when they shouldn't have been there in the first place. The consequences were devastating for him, and he lost sight of everything important in his life, in turn losing Will, his girl at the time.

Oscar's eyes meet mine and a silent acknowledgment passes through us, knowing that he overheard pieces of the conversation via the earpiece. Casting my eyes to the side, Cal sits with his head in his hands, the hurt, and pain obvious among my brothers.

I side-eye Bren, and he nods in understanding before pinching his nose. He glances up at the ceiling and proceeds to take a deep breath. "Okay, so Don said something." All eyes turn to Bren, unable to comprehend there's even more, to add to the turn of events.

"He laughed." My brother's eyes shoot toward me in confusion. "He didn't say it; he laughed it. Gloated, to be precise." I correct Bren, shoving a toothpick into my mouth. If the big dick is going to tell a story, he needs to at least tell it right.

Bren's eyes narrow on me at my correction. His jaw tightens, "You're right. He gloated."

"What did he fucking say?" Impatience screaming from Oscar with his sharp tone at the forefront.

"He said, tell your Ma I know. Tell her I have a surprise for her." Even Bren replaying the words, the sinister edge to them has the hairs on the back of my neck standing to full attention. The fucker is dead and still toying with us from the grave.

"Well, what the fuck does that mean?" Cal quizzes his red-rimmed eyes, searching mine and Bren's for answers.

We look at one another skeptically. If only he'd lasted a little longer, we could have tortured it out of him.

"We need to speak with Ma." Cal interrupts our thoughts.

"No, we fucking don't. You already know she's a head case." I wince. Wow, don't mince your words, Bren. Oscar's spine straightens at Bren's words, making me swallow uncomfortably.

"She's not a fucking head case." Oscar snaps, his face red in temper. He's been called that himself by our father so that one hit home.

"Dick." Con spits out at Bren.

Bren brushes his hand over his head. "Fine. Fuck, not a head case. Just…" Bren lingers, struggling with his words. "She's…" We all watch him. "She's…" He lingers on what to say. Yeah, he's emotionally inept.

"Jesus. She's sensitive. Vulnerable. On edge. Fucking hell,

Bren, it's not difficult." Bren glares back at Cal, the brother most in tune with his emotions out of all of us.

"When do we speak to her?" I ask.

"Sunday. Before dinner. The girls can hang back with Reece and the kids." I nod in agreement.

Con sits forward. "Are we telling them... about Don?" I shuffle uncomfortably.

"No." Oscar and Bren say in unison.

Bren scans all our faces, searching for an argument; he relaxes when he finds none. No, we'll protect our parents from the truth. Nobody needs to know what a monster we had hiding in our family.

When Con killed Will's brother Milo for betraying her, he once said something that stuck with me. "There's a viper in the nest." Only now do I understand what he meant.

The viper in the nest was uncle Don, but we dealt with the viper. We took off his motherfucking head.

CHAPTER 29

Angel

My head pulses, my throat dry. I stutter a gasp, desperate to suck in air. "Shh, it's okay, darlin', I got you." Finn's soothing voice coos from behind me. His head buries into my hair as he inhales my scent. I squeeze my eyes shut, trying to remember what happened. Finn's hold on me tightens.

Memories and images raced through my mind. I told them. Oh god, I told them. My chest heaves, panic coursing through me, and my heart pounds violently against my chest.

An image of Charlie flashes in front of my eyes, realization hitting me painfully in my chest, making me gasp for air. I move to dart up, but Finn's firm grip holds me in place. His warm breath a whisper next to my ear. "Open your eyes, darlin'; she's here. She's here." I whimper against him and open my eyes; my sweet little girl is curled up in a ball beside me.

My body vibrates on its own accord, my heart beating wildly from my chest. "Is she…" My words won't come out. I move my shaking hand toward her and feel her warmth.

As in sensing my thoughts, Finn's gentle voice relaxes me. "She's fine, Angel. Absolutely fine. She's sleeping."

"Did they…?" My body shudders and sickness consumes me. Please tell me they didn't hurt her.

"Shhh… she's been sleeping the whole time. She's fine darlin'."

I roll onto my back to face Finn. His left arm in a sling, my eyes widen, "You're hurt?"

His deep blue eyes sparkle when he chuckles, "Shot. Broken hand too." He holds his arm a little higher.

Is he insane? "Shot?" my eyes bug out.

His hand grazes down my face. "I'm fine, darlin'. It's over."

His words startle me. Replaying in my head. Over? Confusion must mar my face because he reiterates. "Over." His eyes darken with sincerity.

"He's dead?"

"Yeah. Absolutely fucking dead."

Relief spreads through me, causing me to involuntarily whimper.

Finn dips his head and kisses my forehead, his lips lingering. "I'm sorry I let you down."

I watch him. Guilt, his eyes full of guilt. I sigh into his arms, the words leaving me with my everything, "I love you."

His eyes flare with emotion. He chokes a little, his mouth agape. "Yeah?"

"So much it hurts." My fingers find his cheek, trailing down the scruff on his jawline. His eyes screw shut, trying to mask his emotions.

After a few moments, he opens them, swallowing hard. "We going to be a family now? How it shoulda been all along?" His eyebrow raises slightly as if still unsure.

I bite my lip between my teeth, struggling to contain my excitement, his words echoing through my head. "A family, how it shoulda been."

I nod, "Yes."

"Fuck darlin', love you so goddamn much." His mouth crashes into mine. His uninjured hand grasps my jaw firmly, tightening the longer we kiss.

A muffled noise stops us both in our tracks, stilling the passion that was building between us. Our eyes dart toward Charlie, who is slowly stirring from her sleep. Finn climbs off the bed, looking down at me with lusted eyes. "Gonna go make something to eat for my girls." He nods at me, then slowly adjusts his hard-on. My eyes immediately glance at Charlie in a panic, but luckily, she's facing the other opposite way. Finn's loud chuckle fills the room. I narrow my eyes at him before launching a pillow in his direction. Turning on his heels, he leaves the room.

I sink into my pillow, closing my eyes to compose myself.

It's over.

It's finally fucking over.

CHAPTER 30

Finn

It's been two days since we brought princess back to her mama, and we're just on our way to our family estate. Angel, Will and Lily are bringing the kids and Reece over for dinner later, so we have decided to go ahead and break the news to our parents that uncle Don passed away. Shame we can't tell them that we took the sick motherfucker out, but I don't want to hurt my parents more than necessary.

Pulling into the driveway of our parent's home, I swallow back the memories of us growing up here. Our uncle, our hero, would play with us in the gardens, all while my father would bark orders at us. The rope swing still hangs from the tree he would push us on. The treehouse he helped Bren build was still used by Con's son, Keen. How can this man be the same man responsible for selling women and children? The fact that he could be so devious and evil brings another wave of sickness through me.

"You good brother?" Cal's soft voice breaks me out of my memories.

"Yeah, let's get this shit over with." He nods at me in return.

Taking a deep breath, I stroll across the manicured gardens toward the kitchen door. The fresh smell of bread fills my nostrils in preparation for our family meal.

My mother embraces my brothers one after the other, placing a kiss on each cheek and a tight hug that even Oscar receives. Eventually, she reaches me but pauses and looks me in the eye. Her bright blue eyes flash with awareness of some sort. "Finn, what's happened?" I step back slightly, taken aback by her motherly instinct.

"Ma, come sit down so we can explain," Cal speaks softly to ma, steering her into her chair by her elbow.

Da is already sitting at the table. Right at the top as the head of the house with ma at the opposite end. Oscar sits next to Ma. He has done since he was a small child, with him being a little different from us. Ma always kept him close. Cal and Bren sit opposite one another on either side of Da. Bren being the oldest and Cal second in line to the family business, they've always endured the harshness of our father's expectations of them; me and Con sit down at the bottom end of the table near ma.

"What the feck is going on now?" Da spits out the words like venom. His broad shoulders tighten with tension. I glance at Bren and sure enough, his do the same. He's a younger version of our father. There's no mistaking that, however, where Da has the family's thick, dark hair, Bren has shaved his short as if separating himself from the rest of us.

"Got some sad news." Bren's voice doesn't sound remotely sad nor sorry. I stare at the table in front of me, my hands clasped together, a toothpick hanging from my mouth.

"Spit it the feck out, then." Da all but bellows. I hear Oscar sigh at Da's impatience.

"It's Don. He's dead." Bren's voice is empty of any emotion. Typical fucking Bren.

Da sucks in a deep breath. I register him shaking from the corner of my eye, but I refuse to acknowledge his reaction.

I flick my eyes up toward ma and see her staring at the table much like I was. She's no doubt in shock, given that Don has always been such a major part of all our lives.

"How?" Da's voice sounds far away, almost broken, completely unlike the man we know and respect.

Bren clears his throat and shifts from side to side, not comfortable having to lie to protect the son of a bitch. But this is for Da. I swallow away the feeling of resentment.

"Shoot out with the Russians. Igor Dimitriev is dead too." He relays our story nonchalantly, with no compassion what-soever, I wouldn't expect any other from him, I guess.

I scan my eyes over Da. His shoulders slackened, his face blank, and he nods his head in understanding. We sit in silence around the table, everyone deep in thought. Well, I guess that went better than expected.

Cal clears his throat, cutting through the silence. "Finn has something to tell you. Something good." He eyes our parents pointedly.

Ma's eyes dart to mine, alight with intrigue, picking up on her reaction to me earlier. "I brought you a present to dinner Ma." Her eyes narrow slightly in confusion. I smile at her, my whole-body lighting up. "Found Angel Ma, brought her home." Ma gasps, her shaky hand going to her mouth.

"Where the feck she been?" Da spits out angrily. I turn on him in an instant, all thoughts of sympathy for him going out the fucking window the moment the fucker's tone changed. Lurching from my chair and moving toward him, Bren blocks my passage, pushing me back in my chair. Anger swirls inside me at the audacity of the old cunt, speaking badly about my girl. I point,

"I'm warning ya, you old bastard. You upset my girl, and I'll pop a bullet in your fucking head, understand me?"

"Finn…" Ma's soft, caring voice soothes me as she runs her hand over my arm. "Where's she been all this time?" Her eyes implore me to explain, but I squeeze them shut to block out the guilt of lying to Ma.

"She's done well for herself and has a little girl now," Oscar replies before I screw up what we rehearsed.

"A daughter?" Ma's eyes fill with love. The muscles in my shoulders relax and I sink back into my chair.

"Yeah, she's amazing, Ma. Her name's Charlie."

Ma's eyes glisten with tears. "I can't wait to see them, sweetheart." I smile and nod at ma, her warmth filling me with pride.

Until the old fucker opens his mouth, "How old's the kid?" I bristle at his words.

"Almost eight." Bren answers, and I close my eyes, knowing Da is doing the math in his head.

"She cheated on you?" His voice sounds as shocked and disappointed as I was when I first realized how old my princess was. But now I know the truth. I'm livid because, let's face it. What the fuck does it have to do with him?

"She ain't welcome here if she cheated on you. You dumb fucker, you always were head over feckin heels for that girl, following her around like a sap. Well, no feckin way am I playing happy families, no feckin way." He bashes his fist on the table; the vibrations felt all the way at the bottom. No doubt taking his shitty news and pouring his emotions out, using Angel as an excuse. Not going to happen.

My heart beats rapidly in my chest, the beast threatening to come out. I palm my fists beside me, and then the fucker makes the biggest error he could possibly make. His words cut into me, the hurt and rage more than anyone could ever imagine. "A whore just like her mother."

I fly from my chair, unhook the blade from my boot and throw it down on the table right beside Da's shaking hand. My foot pushes off the fallen chair, giving me the perfect step to launch myself up on the table and propel myself to the sack of shit that dared to dis my girl. Bren tackles me down on the table, the impact making me wince against my injured arm and hand. "Calm the fuck down, Finn. He doesn't know, brother; he doesn't know." Bren's voice whispers into my ear, attempting to calm me as I struggle against him, determined to strangle the life out of Da.

"Angel has never cheated on Finn, Da. Their relationship is complicated and has nothing to do with us. She'll be welcomed here and respected as she deserves, understand me?" Cal's no-nonsense voice takes us all by surprise. I struggle to lift my seething head from the table to stare directly into Da's eyes.

"Of course, she will, won't she, Brennan." Ma chimes in, trying to ease the atmosphere.

"Yeah, and if it's a fucking problem, it's the last you'll see of us all," Con adds.

"No problem. Is there Brennan?" Ma implores, staring at her husband. It's rare Ma says anything against Da, so he must see something in her pleading eyes that resonates because I witness the defeat leave his body.

He rolls his lip between his teeth. "Fine. They're welcome." His words come out pissed and despondent, "Now someone get me a feckin drink, my brother has died."

My body sags in relief. Just let the fucker go back on his word. He'll wish it was him dead if he hurts my girls.

CHAPTER 31

Angel

    I'm extremely clingy toward Charlie, and I know it's annoying her, but I can't seem to help myself. Whenever she leaves the room, I feel the need to follow her, just to make sure she's okay, and safe. I have to stop myself from double-checking the bathroom when she goes in there.

The past two nights, she's slept with Finn and me, but after realizing it's aggravating her and the fact that me and Finn are struggling to keep our hands off one another, I've decided today she can sleep in her own bed tonight, but I'm not going to pretend it doesn't unnerve me. I face timed Tyler this morning and gave him a full rundown of what had happened while Finn took Charlie to see Keen. They've become good friends since, and it's endearing to see her build a bond with Finn's family members.

"When is Sam coming to take us to dinner?" Charlie asks again for the hundredth time.

I sigh and place my cup on the kitchen counter before glancing at my watch. "Ten minutes."

She jumps up and down, making her blonde locks float around her pretty little face. Since Sam helped aid Charlie's rescue, she's become a little obsessed with him. It's cute to see, but the poor guy is as uncomfortable as hell.

When the buzzer sounds, Charlie squeals an ear-piercing squeal and flies toward the door. "Check the security camera!" I chastise before she opens the door. Her body stills, then she goes through the motions of checking the screen before deeming it safe to open the door. She doesn't know that she was kidnapped, but she definitely senses something has happened to her; she knows I'm being overtly clingy, and as always, she humors me but I also know she can feel that there's more to it than just my usual paranoia.

"I did all the steps, Mommy," she smiles back over her shoulder at me, and I give her a thumbs up for her to open the door.

———

The car comes to a stop at Finn's family home. Before I know what's happening, the door to the car opens and Finn's hand encompasses mine, pulling me out of the car and into his chest. The sound of his heart beating rapidly through his shirt. He nuzzles his mouth into my hair, dropping a kiss on my head, "Missed you so much darlin'." I smile into his chest at his sweet words. We've only been apart for a few hours.

"Finn, can I sit next to you at dinner?" Charlie asks.

"Sure, princess, you can sit wherever you like." Charlie grins up at Finn like he's her hero; unbeknownst to her, he actually is. Mine too.

"You gonna go find Keen, then join us inside?" Finn asks Charlie, who's now scanning the gardens and eyeing up the play structure with Reece chasing a laughing Keen around. Charlie doesn't even answer. She runs off without a backward glance. Her confidence and sweet personality fill me with pride.

"You ready for this, darlin'?" Finn's eyes implore mine, his uninjured hand tightening gently on my chin, forcing me to stare into his eyes. I nod. His lips swoop down and take mine, his tongue sweeping in. Finn's hand tightens on my jaw. I throw my arms around his neck, and he pushes his hard body into me, grinding against me, showing me how hard he is for me.

"Finn! Put her the fuck down and get your ass inside. Ma is climbing the fucking walls waiting." Bren bellows across the garden. I step back and nibble my lip to stifle my laugh. "You're fuckin gorgeous; you know that?" Finn's heavily lusted eyes hold me in place, my heart beating heavier at his words. I feel so lucky to know he still wants me. After everything that has happened, he still wants me.

He tugs my hand in his uninjured one and pulls me along toward the house. My heart beats faster with each step, both excited with anticipation and nervous at seeing Brennan and Cyn again after so long. Will they hate me for leaving? For hurting Finn.

Finn opens the door, and the familiar scent surrounds me. The emotions roll through my bloodstream, memories of helping Cyn in the kitchen. She was like the mother I never had, mine the junkie whore and Cyn the homemaker, welcoming both Will and me into her family unit with warm, loving, open arms.

No sooner do I step foot into the kitchen than Cyn throws herself at me, her tight grip choking me. Her tears fall as fast as mine. "Shh," she coos as we both openly sob. Her arms braced around me slowly, transforming into the same comforting swirling motion on my spine that Finn uses. Only now do I recognize it as something his mother must have taught him. I squeeze my eyes closed, willing myself to stay upright and in control, but it's a battle I'm losing. My sobs increase. "It's okay, my child, you're here now. Finn has got you. We've all got you."

Eventually, Cyn eases back to look at me. She's slightly

taller than me, so she gazes down at me, assessing the changes in my appearance and body. Her blue eyes falter when they meet mine, and I glance away, swallowing thickly at the guilt surrounding the lies around Don's death. She seems to recognize my reluctance to be completely open. Holding my chin gently in her hand, she tilts my head up to look at her. I squeeze my eyes shut. "Angel, sweetie. Look at me." I shake my head in response. I register Finn's hand on my lower back, his chest behind me. A tower of support. He kisses the top of my head, "You got this darlin'."

I open my eyes and see the sympathy and love cascading from Cyn's eyes. No hate or malice, just pure love. I throw my arms around her again, taking in her scent.

"Angel. Welcome home." My spine straightens at Brennan's booming voice, startling me. I turn my head to the left and find Brennan looking down on mine and Cyn's interaction with affection before he transforms his features, "Break my boy's heart and I'll…"

"You shut your fucking mouth right now before I take your tongue out, old man!" Finn practically screams.

I place my hand on Finn's chest, right over his heart, to calm him down. "It's okay, Finn. I'm not going anywhere."

His eyes meet mine, becoming a little hooded. He licks his lips and dips his head to kiss me, his voice low and sensual. "Damn fucking right, you ain't darlin'. Gonna knock you up and put a ring on your finger." My eyebrows shoot up in surprise, making him chuckle. "You think you're pregnant now? Think my cum this morning filled you up with my baby?" My eyes scan around the room quickly, my cheeks heating at his dirty words. Please tell me his parents aren't hearing this.

CHAPTER 32

Finn

Watching the interaction between Angel and my Ma choked me up. I could feel the love pouring from them both. My cold, brutal heart warms at my girl, being where she belongs, where she always belonged.

I scan my woman's body. Hot as fuck in her tight jeans, her tits pulling against her t-shirt. I made her change this morning because she put a white one on. I wasn't sitting around the table with my brothers, knowing they might catch a glimpse of my girl's tits or piercings. No fucking way. She can save that shit for me.

This cherry red hair has got to go too. It's hot and all, but I want that part of my Angel back; besides Charlie has the same color and my girls need to flaunt their gorgeous locks. My hand tightens on Angel's hip. She leans against me slightly, causing her ass to rub against my cock. I'm on a mission to knock her up and lock her up with a ring on her finger, ensuring she's mine forever, where she belongs.

Con is desperate to marry Will, but he wants this big, elaborate wedding to show off. Me? I just want my girl to say she's mine, slap a ring on her, and kill any fucker that dares to look her way. Maybe I should take her to Vegas? I'll get Oscar to see if there are any flights, preferably tomorrow. I lick my lips, excitement bouncing off me.

"Angel. Welcome home." Angel's spine straightens at my da's deep voice. Anger floods my veins for him, making my girl jump. Fucking prick. "Break my boy's heart and I'll…"

I shut him down before he can say another fucking word. My blood boils and my temple pulsates. "You shut your fucking mouth right now before I take your tongue out, old man!"

Angel puts her hand over my heart, instantly calming me. "It's okay Finn. I'm not going anywhere." Her soft voice reassures me. Her words repeating in my mind, "not going anywhere."

Her eyes meet mine and desire flows through me. I need her right fucking now. I need her. Licking my lips, I duck my head to place a soft kiss on those strawberry lips; I keep my voice low, so my parents can't hear. "Damn fucking right, you ain't darlin'. Gonna knock you up and put a ring on your finger." Angel's eyebrows jump in shock, and I can't help but throw my head back and laugh at her innocent reaction. "You think you're pregnant now? Think my cum this morning filled you up with my baby?" My dick throbs against my jeans, pre-cum dampening my boxers. Motherfucker, I need her.

The door swings open with a boom, making all eyes turn in that direction. Reece struts into the kitchen. "Are we fucking eating today or not?" He looks pissed.

He throws himself on his chair and pulls his phone out, tapping away, completely oblivious to anything else happening around him.

A soft giggle from behind lets me know princess has entered the room, swiftly followed by the commotion of everyone else arriving. "Reece isn't happy because Uncle Cal told him he's not allowed to pay for a prom date." I grin at

Charlie's words. The fact she's already calling Cal uncle fills me with pride. It won't be long until she calls me dad, and I can't fucking wait. I'll erase every god damn memory before me and make both her and Angel my own in no time.

"Let me see you, sweetie." Ma's voice cuts through my thoughts. She pushes past me slightly and bends down to greet Charlie.

Ma lets out a gasp that fills the room. Her hands shake as she stares into Charlie's eyes. Charlie is frozen, not responding. Her lip trembles and I feel myself becoming irritated at the fact that Ma is upsetting her. My tone darkens without intent. "Ma, you're scaring her."

Ma's pale face turns toward me, my stomach somersaults. "Her... her eyes Finn." I swallow thickly at her words. Surely, she doesn't know. She can't know, right? Ma points down at Charlie, Angel moving quickly, putting herself in front of her. "Her eyes." Ma grabs her rosary beads, clutching them tightly. Her face filled with terror.

She stumbles. I put out my hand to catch her, but she catches onto the dining chair instead.

Her voice sounds hollow as though she's talking to herself, "He... he wouldn't. He didn't." She gasps again as we all watch her in horror. Ma's shaking hand goes to her mouth. "My sweet girl." She stumbles toward Angel, but I stand, and pull her into my side protectively. "It's... it's all my fault. It's my fault." She gets louder and louder with each word. "I should have stopped him." Her next words shocked me to my core. "I should have known he'd do it again."

"Reece, take the kids outside now!" Cal shouts from somewhere behind us.

"Fuck off!" Reece snipes back, not even lifting his head from his phone. The whole room is holding their breath on Ma's meltdown and Reece isn't in the least bit phased.

"NOW!" Cal screams at him.

Reece huffs and pushes his chair back, mumbling words

of profanity as he leaves the room. Angel gently coaxes Charlie to go with Reece. Her reluctant eyes penetrate into mine. I nod at her in approval, and she gives me an uncertain smile, leaving the room with the click of the door.

"Cyn, sit down and tell us what the feck is happenin'," Da grumbles.

Ma's shaky body is helped into her chair by Will and Lily, both kneeling on either side of her with concern.

Cal kneels down in front of ma. "Somebody tell me what the feck is happening." Da paces the room.

Cal ignores da and takes ma's hand. "Ma, you said you should have stopped him from doing it again. Who Ma?"

Ma's eyes dart to my da and my blood runs cold. "Did he fuckin touch you?" Bren pushes through us. "Did that sick fuck hurt you too?" His face twisted in rage. Bren's chest rises and falls rapidly, irritation oozing from him.

Ma's voice is so soft it's almost a whisper. "Yes."

The room goes deathly silent, only gasps clipping the air. Angel whimpers beside me, and I feel her whole-body shudder. I tug her even closer to me.

"Who feckin touched ya?" Da pushes past Bren and stands towering above Cal. "Who did it, Cyn?" His hands push through his hair in aggravation.

Ma closes her eyes tightly and shakes her head. She breathes out loudly and straightens her shoulders, lifts her head up, and stares da straight in the eyes. "Don."

We all stiffen in response to her words. The room seems smaller. My heart beats faster. Angel drops her head into my chest and my hand automatically holds her head there, cradling her weeping body into my chest.

"Son of a fucking bitch!" Bren booms, upturning a coffee table.

"Bren, calm the fuck down." Con spits out.

Bren's solid body heaves up and down.

Da stands tall, spins on his heels, and then glares at me

before casting his eyes down toward Angel. I tighten my arm protectively around her. His eyes soften before he raises his chin at me. Understanding crosses over his face; his eyes penetrate mine. "You make him suffer?"

I nod, "Yeah."

He gives me a nod back in respect, then moves around the table and sits in his chair.

All our eyes follow him. Clearing his throat, he begins to talk.

CHAPTER 33

Finn

We wait with bated breath, all eyes locked on da, waiting for him to explain something. Anything.

He clears his throat. "I worked away a lot." We all nod, remembering how da worked away organizing the business while Don would hold down the fort, managing the warehouses.

"Before Oscar was born, I came home, and your ma wasn't the same." His voice goes off in the distance as we listen to his version of events. "I thought she was pissed, me working away, her holding down a house with two little ones. About eight weeks later, she told me she was pregnant." His voice turns darker. "Knew it wasn't feckin mine. Hadn't been anywhere near her." I bristle at his tone. "She broke down and told me someone hurt her." I wince, cradling Angel closer to me, needing her as much as she needs me. "Said someone broke into the house while I was away."

My mind goes over the whispers of my brothers over the years: Bren telling me ma was pregnant but never had the baby.

"He was drunk." Ma's wavering voice tells us. "He'd

221

never been inappropriate before." She wrings her hands in her apron. "He attacked me and the next day acted as though nothing had happened." Her lip wobbles, "I couldn't tell your father. Couldn't break his heart. I thought maybe he was too drunk to know better."

"Ma!" Bren snaps. "He's a fuckin rapist."

Her eyes flare. "I know that, Bren. You don't think I know that? Believe me; I watched that man like a hawk around my family. I never saw a glimpse of the man I saw that night. I was scared, Bren. Scared of the consequences, scared your Da would accuse me of things."

My eyebrows knit together in confusion. "What do you mean, Ma?" Cal asks her diplomatically. "Your Da thought I was having an affair because we'd not…" She pauses and looks down at her hands embarrassed, "been intimate."

Bren's nostrils flare, and we all glare at da accusingly. "Told ya I was feckin sorry for that." He points at ma.

She stands tall on her feet and points her own finger back at da, across the table. "And I told you I forgive you, but not your actions, Brennan, not your words." Will jumps from her crouching position, and something crosses over ma and Will's faces, some sort of mutual understanding between them.

Da drops his head into his hands, no doubt in shame.

"What happened to the baby?" Oscar asks out of the blue.

Da's voice comes out irritated. "Told her she could keep it, told her I'd raise him as my own."

"Him?" Cal stands up, and Lily goes to him to comfort him. All of us are on one side of the table and da on the other.

Ma pulls the small teddy from her apron and strokes it gently, looking down at it with a maternal smile. "We told everyone I'd gone to stay with family for a couple of months. I went to stay at a retreat near Boston. You boys came with me until I was far enough to give birth." She smiles solemnly at Bren and Cal. "I had him on a Friday morning. Theodore O'Connell.

He was chunky with rosy cheeks and a good set of lungs. Teddy, I nicknamed him Teddy." She laughs to herself emptily. Pieces of the jigsaw over the years begin to come together. Whenever ma got stressed or upset, she'd pull the soft toy from her pocket. We always assumed she was referring to the stuffed toy as being "Teddy," not a literal baby, her baby. Our brother.

"You didn't lose him?" Cal questions.

"No. I gave him up for adoption." Her lip trembles as she gazes around at each one of us. "How could I keep him? He'd have known he wasn't ya Da's. Then what?"

Cal moves toward ma and pulls her into his embrace, placing a kiss on her head.

Bren fidgets from foot to foot. "Ma, there's something you need to know."

"Not now, Bren." Cal snaps.

Ma's head pops up, determination in her words. "Now, we get it all out in the open; then we move on. As a family." She holds out her hand for Angel, and I watch as my girl seeks comfort in my mother's arms.

I stand behind them both with my uninjured arm over them.

Bren hesitates before swallowing hard and staring into ma's eyes. "Before Don died. He said, tell your Ma I know. Tell her I have a surprise for her."

Ma falls with a wail from deep inside her, both me and Angel too slow to catch her.

"Please, no. No, no."

Da jumps up from the chair. "Cyn. It's okay, I told ya. Got him a good home, where he's safe."

"Da, I need details on where you placed him. I need to look into it all." Oscar stares at our father with intensity. Da gives Oscar a nod.

"Lily, Will, can you take ma to her room?" Cal asks softly. They both help ma up from the floor.

Angel grips my shirt, her eyes imploring me, "Can we go home, Finn? Please." Her whole-body was overwhelmed.

I kiss her forehead. "Yeah, darling. Gonna take you and princess home."

I gaze at Oscar, who is staring into space. "Let me know if you find anything out." He nods without looking at me. I pick Angel up bridal style and place a gentle kiss on her head. Her familiar strawberry scent invades my nostrils, and my protective instincts tighten around her.

CHAPTER 34

Angel

Finn collected us take out while I had a bath in his enormous suite. My body was completely drained from the day's events. Charlie fell to sleep on the couch shortly after finishing her dinner, so Finn carried her to bed.

Peering up from the sink, I place my toothbrush back in its holder and stare at myself in the mirror. My eyes catch on to the tattoos running down my arm to cover the physical marks I left on myself after the mental scars became too much to bear. I grimace at the thought. The hurt and trauma that monster has put us through. So many secrets and lies. But I'm standing here now, with Finn and our family beside me, ready to embark on our new journey together like we always should have been. I couldn't be prouder of the boy I fell in love with, the man he's become. I know he has a dark side, but I don't care. He'll always be the boy I loved, the boy I gave my heart to when we were just kids.

"Darlin', you fuckin lost in there?" Finn's voice echoes through the wall. I stifle a laugh. Shaking my head, I pull down on the short negligee and walk toward the bedroom with a sway of my hips.

Finn is sitting upright in bed with his good arm behind his head. His eyes find mine immediately, and a cocky smile spreads over his face.

"Holy fuckin hell, darlin'." He whistles through his teeth. "We ain't going to sleep, right?" He quirks a brow, and I tug my lip in between my teeth to stop myself from giggling.

I crawl onto the bed.

"Fuck." Finn shuffles on the bed, then proceeds to throw off the comforter, exposing his naked form. His good hand moves toward his cock, and he begins to stroke himself. "Fuck, darlin', lose the sexy dress. Need to see your tits and pussy." His dirty mouth makes my body pulsate. I tug the negligee over my head, exposing my bare body to him. "Fuck, darlin', fuck." He pants the words out, his hand moving faster. I move my own hand to between my legs and begin circling my clit, gently adding a little more pressure before easing off. With my left hand, I play with my nipple, gently massaging it around my piercing.

My eyes never leave Finn's, his heavy, needing eyes completely enthralled in me, making my whole-body alight with excitement and need.

"You want me to fuck you, darlin'? Fuck you hard."

I can barely get the words out, "Yes." I swallow, "Yes, please."

Finn leaps forward, grabs my arm, and throws me onto the bed. "Damn fucking right you do. Show me how wet you are for me, Angel." I show him my fingers, glistening with arousal. "Suck 'em off, darlin'." I do as he asks, placing both fingers in my mouth. Finn's pupils dilate at the action. He shuffles up the bed slightly, positioning himself between my legs.

He dips his head down to kiss me while his hand rubs his cock around my opening and back up around my clit. The swift jerking of his cock against my opening makes my breathing stagger, and the need to feel him inside of me desperate. I lift my hips when his cock comes into contact with my opening, but he chuckles and moves it away, tugging fast and hard on his cock, teasing me.

"Does my dirty Angel want my cock?" There's a playfulness about him.

I smack his good arm. "You know I do. Now give it to me, or I'll finish myself off." I taunt. His hand moves away from between my legs. He places it around my throat and tightens it slightly.

"Like fuck you will, darlin'. Not unless I let ya. It's my pussy to take care of, you hear me?"

I nod slightly because of the restrictive hold on me. "Good girl, now ask me nicely to fuck this pussy full of cum." He licks his lips and watches me closely to see if I'll obey.

"Please, Finn. Please fill me with your cum."

He thrusts forward, barely giving me the chance to finish the sentence. His hard thrust knocking me up the bed as he powers into me. "Fuck yeah. Clench that pussy like that darlin'."

The rhythm of his thrusts and the rubbing of his body against me bring a pool of wetness between my legs. "Please, Finn."

"What darlin'? Please, what?"

"Please fill me with your cum."

His eyes latch onto mine. "You want my baby, don't you?" He grits the words out as if struggling to hold himself together. "Fucking say it, Angel!"

I cling onto his muscular body, my nails digging into his back. I hold on as he hammers into me, my orgasm fast approaching.

"Yes, please, yes. Please fill me with your cum. Give me a baby."

"Fffuuccck… fuck!" Finn screeches out, throwing his head

back as the throbbing of his cock pulls my own orgasm from me. Waves of euphoria hit me as Finn's hard body continues to relentlessly pound into me before collapsing on top of me, completely spent.

"I love you, darlin'." Our lips meet before I pull back slightly.

"I love you too."

Finn grins in response. "Damn fucking right you do, I think I just knocked you the fuck up." He chuckles but doesn't move off me. His eyes roam over my naked body. His cock hardens when his eyes lock on to my piercings. He ducks his head and sucks a nipple into my mouth. I grip the bedsheets beside me in my fists and embrace the stirring sensations arising inside me once again. Closing my eyes, I feel the complete and utter devotion as Finn begins making love to me.

CHAPTER 35

F our weeks later

Finn

We're gathered around the table for our usual Sunday dinner at our parents' house. Since all the secrets and lies came out, we've been over here multiple times now. Both Angel and Charlie are completely at ease and comfortable here. My da has even taken a protective stance over them both.

"How's the wedding planning coming on, Will?" Ma asks Will, who sits with her hand in Con's on the table.

"Good. Con wants Peppa to wear a little doggie suit."

Da chokes on his food. "Ya feckin what? Jesus feckin Christ. The dog is a feckin pansy, and now my son is one too." He points his dinner knife in Con's direction.

Con's head whirls around so fast it's a wonder he doesn't get whiplash. "Call my fucking dog a pansy again and see what happens!" He spits back. I chuckle to myself that da can call him a pansy, but not his dog.

"Reece, did you ask your date to the prom?" Will asks Reece as if changing the subject on purpose, a seething Con still glaring our father down.

Reece refuses to lift his head from his meal and continues on as if to ignore her question completely. "No, but she's coming." My eyes catch on to Cal, who sighs in defeat against his chair. They flick back at Oscar, who grimaces knowingly. What the fuck is going on there?

Lily chooses that moment to change the subject yet again, "So Chloe can now walk completely unaided," she smiles down at their toddler daughter in the highchair, who's currently trying to feed herself. "She's determined to get to Puss." Lily sighs.

"It's because everyone loves pussy!" Keen announces, making us all stifle our grins, his innocent words now becoming a regular occurrence at the dinner table. My eyes flit over to the fluffy tortoiseshell cat in question. It's sat on the table beside Reece and the rat bastard dog Peppa. Con said the bold-haired fucker is a Chinese crested, but I think someone sold him a dud.

"Did you ask Marianne as a date for the wedding?" Oscar asks Bren.

Bren's fork stops close to his mouth, but he doesn't make eye contact with anyone before he shoves another mouthful in. Leaving us all waiting for his response.

A clipped, "No."

Oscar sighs. "Bren, she's going to be pissed. What have I told you about keeping her sweet?"

Bren sits up straight. His eyes glare toward Oscar. He points his fork in his direction. "You're the one that tells me not to mess women around."

Oscar holds his eyes. "Her father is becoming angsty."

Bren lifts his chin. "Let him."

Oscar's hands shake on the table. "You sure about that?" He raises an eyebrow in question.

The room was filling with tension.

"Not having no pussy, tell me what to do." Bren's eyes narrow on Oscar's, waiting for an argument. "Gonna pay for a date like you pay when you want a woman." Bren taunts.

"Daddy, can me and Keen give Pussy some fish?" Charlie's sweet voice fills the room and cuts off the awkward atmosphere building.

I glance down at my little girl, her rosy cheeks beaming back up at me, her words filling me with pride. "Sure, sweetheart, whatever you want."

Reece scoffs, causing my eyes to shoot up toward his. "They mean fish out of the pond, you dumb fuck." Reece tilts his head toward the outside door.

Oh shit.

"Charlie, you're not taking fish from the pond, sweetheart." Angel soothes Charlie. "Besides, I've got something to tell you, all of you." She sits straighter in her chair.

My eyebrows furrow in confusion, and she meets my eyes; the beautiful smile gracing her face makes me return her smile.

"So, as you may have heard, Finn's been desperate for a baby."

I sit back in my chair and grin to myself; damn fucking right I'm desperate for a baby and happy for everyone to know it. My cock fills my woman up good, and will have no problem giving her a few kids.

"Well, he's got what he wanted. I'm pregnant." I glance at her, her lip caught in her teeth. She watches me closely for a reaction.

Wait a minute, did I just hear her right?

Is she for real?

As if hearing my thoughts, she nods. I scan her body from top to toe and land on her stomach; my eyes shoot back up to hers. My heart hammers in my chest. Is it true? "You knocked up?"

Her smile widens at my shocked words, "Yes."

I lunge forward, taking her chin between my forefingers as I cover her mouth with my own, completely ignoring everyone else in the room. I pull back when we both begin panting, resting my forehead against hers. Love seeps through her eyes into my soul, deep into my scarred heart, filling me with an explosion of love for them both. Our family.

"I'm going to be a big sister?" Charlie shrieks from beside me, a squeal almost deafening me, making me chuckle in response to her reaction.

Excitement fills the room, congratulations and praises are passed around. The women hug. Ma and Angel cry when they embrace one another.

It's the best news I've ever heard in my entire fucking life.

I finally have my family.

My forever.

EPILOGUE

Four weeks later

Finn

I open the door to my brother Bren's apartment, agreeing to a poker night when all I wanna do is slide in between my girl's thighs. I'm the last to arrive, and a little late, they've already started the game. I stroll over to the table and sit down, grabbing a beer and popping the top.

"Nice of you to join us." Oscar's deadpan voice quips.

"Choke on a bag of dicks, you miserable bastard," I reply and throw a chip at his face. "I've got a woman that's knocked up and needed a fucking foot rub." I glare at him.

"Foot rub?" Con queries as though making a mental note. He sits at the table looking a real bell end with that mangy little rat sitting on his knee. Will makes him bring it out because the damn dog has separation anxiety from him and leaves nervous shits everywhere whenever Con goes out.

"Can't believe Angel is knocked up already." Cal chuckles. I sit back in my chair proudly, arms behind my head.

"What can I say? Fucking monster cock and super sperm. I've got it all, brother." I wink at my brother for emphasis.

"Yeah, with a fucking pea brain." Bren grunts without looking at me. His eyes are transfixed on his cards.

"Soon as me and Will are married, I'm knocking her up." Con grins to himself like a child.

I side-eye, my little brother. "You should just fuck off to Vegas like me and Angel did. I don't know why the fuck you need to spend a shit ton of green on one fucking day."

Con sighs as though he's talking to his kid. "Because dipshit, my woman wants a proper wedding, so I'm giving her what she wants." He shrugs nonchalantly.

Bren scoffs, "Please, that's the biggest pile of shit I ever heard. You wanted the fucking big elaborate wedding, not Will. Will couldn't give a shit; the poor fucking woman is just going along with you, so you don't have another fucking meltdown."

Con's eyes bug out at Bren's choice of words. I notice Cal's spine straighten as if ready for battle. Con stays perfectly still, and I hold my fucking breath, waiting for his reaction. "What the fuck ever? So, what if I want to show the world who owns Will? Let some fucker try to steal her, see how far he gets." He lifts a shoulder as though what he's saying is completely normal and makes perfect sense.

Bren chuckles, "You're getting married because you want people to know Will is yours? You have any idea how deranged you sound right now?"

Con pulls a childish face back at Bren. "Don't fucking care." He glares into his eyes. "You just wait brother, one day, you're going to be as possessive as us." He waves his hands in mine and Cal's direction.

Bren scoffs, "Fucking doubtful. I just need a hole to empty my load into, not all this other shit." He waves his hand around the table.

"How noble of you." Oscar seethes at Bren's choice of words.

Bren sits back, his huge, muscled shoulders bulging in his shirt; his deep blue eyes point directly at Oscar, "About as noble as you paying for sex." Bren crosses his arms over his chest as if preparing for an argument, raising an eyebrow at Oscar.

I decide to change the subject before my brothers start an all-out, unnecessary war with one another.

"Are we any closer to figuring out who the Mexican guy is that attacked Angel?" I lick my lips and take a swig of my beer, desperate to quench my dry throat. The same reaction occurs whenever we discuss what happened to Angel.

The mood turns solemn in an instant.

Oscar sits straighter. "Not exactly. I'm working through Don's computer files. There's…" he's quiet for a moment before he begins talking again, swallowing deeply. "A lot of fucked up shit on there."

I nod in understanding, a sickening feeling swirling around inside my stomach.

"What about Teddy?" Cal asks, fidgeting uncomfortably. I don't know why the fuck he's so desperate to find him. Annoyance bubbles inside me.

"I'm getting closer," Oscar admits.

"Maybe we should leave it alone." I throw it out there without looking at my brothers as I peel the label off my beer.

Cal all but fucking gasps in my direction. "He's our brother, Finn!"

I glare at him. "Like fuck he is; he's that fucking rapist's son. Probably fucked in the head, just like him." I stare at him defiantly, begging him to argue.

"Like Charlie, you mean?" Bren spits out.

My shoulders tighten, and my head whips around in his direction. He holds his hands up. "Just fucking saying, brother. She's biologically Don's, same as Teddy."

My eyes drill into him. "She's fucking mine."

Bren nods, "Get that. But she's innocent, the same as him. What about Ma, huh? You think this is fair to her? She deserves to know her kid, Finn, just like Angel got to know hers." I play his words over in my mind. I know he's right. I drag a hand down my face. Fuck, I know he's right. Just because he created him doesn't mean this Teddy dude is the same as him. "Yeah, I get it." I reluctantly spit out.

Bren's cell phone cuts through the increasing tension in the room. He mouths, "warehouse," to Oscar. "Put it on speaker." Bren nods and puts the cell on the table. I glance at Con, who is now feeding his bold rat bastard chips. I look away from my little brother, shaking my head. Bren's words are still replaying in my mind.

"Have you opened it?" Bren's voice booms, bringing me back to the present.

"No, sir. I don't think it's one of ours. It has a blue sticker on the side." The hairs on the back of my neck rise at the mention of the blue sticker. All my brothers' eyes direct at me, assessing me for a reaction.

"Give me a full breakdown of the situation." Oscar sits forward.

"The shipment came in on time, sir. But this crate stood out because when we weighed it, it was under the weight requirement."

"By how much?" Oscar's eyebrows knit together.

My hands twitch beside me, unease racing through me.

"The crate weighs seven hundred and twenty pounds, sir."

We all glance at one another, all but Oscar, who is staring at the phone. He blinks as if something is registering in his brain.

"We'll be there in fifteen minutes. Do not touch the crate. Do you understand?"

"Yes, sir."

The line goes dead.

I lick my lips and wait for Oscar's response. "I think it's a person in the crate."

"What?" Cal gasps.

"What the fuck makes you think that?" Bren glares at Oscar in disbelief.

"An average crate is five hundred and fifty pounds. An average person is one hundred and seventy, coupled with the fact it has a blue fucking sticker on the side. I'm pretty damn sure there's a person in the crate."

"Jesus!" Bren scrubs his hand down his face. My heart races in my chest, a desperate need to maim someone boiling at the surface.

"What we gonna do?" Con asks while standing with the dog.

Bren is already reattaching his gun holster. "Gonna go check it out. Oscar, keep the feds off our back." Oscar nods and begins working on his tablet.

"I'm coming with you," I tell him as I check my Glock.

"You sure you can handle it?" Bren's eyes meet mine knowingly. Knowing I'm potentially walking into a similar setup to what Angel was in. Fury rushes through my veins, anger clogging in my throat. "Of course." I nod in his direction, determined to get some answers about what's inside the crate or who.

We might have cut off the head of the snake, but its venom still lives on, that's for fucking sure.

THE END

AFTERWORD

Want a little more?

Would you like more of Finn and Angel?

Come and sign up to BJ Alpha's newsletter for an exclusive extra scene and be the first to hear about the up-and-coming events and book news.

Use the link to get your copy of Finn and Angels extended epilogue now:

Extended Epilogue

ACKNOWLEDGMENTS

I must start with where it all began, TL Swan. When I started reading your books, I never realized I was in a place I needed pulling out of. Your stories brought me back to myself.

With your constant support and the network created as 'Cygnet Inkers' I was able to create something I never realized was possible, I genuinely thought I'd had my day. You made me realize tomorrow is just the beginning.

For that I am eternally grateful!

Tee, thank you for everything.
Thank you for giving me purpose.

To my fellow Cygnets, thank you all so very much.

Again, Jaclyn for always encouraging me, your support is incredible.

Kerry for always being there, even when she's on her hols.

Vicki and Sadie for all your advice and quick responses. Thank you for showing me the way when I needed it. I'm counting down for our first meet.

Thank you to my Beta Readers, Libby, Rhi, Jaclyn, Kate and Heather. I'm so thankful for your help and constant support.

Again, a special thank you to Libby.

A special mention to the Swan Squad.

This group of ladies are incredible and forcing my acknowledgements to grow with each book.

Emma H, Patricia B, Claire B, Caroline W, Anita, Sue and the amazing Bren with her swan cnuts, thank you all for your constant friendship and support.

My beautiful friends.

My banging beauties; Kate and Emma, I love you ladies so very much, thank you for your constant support and daily laughs.

Kate, thank you for being my go-to in every aspect of my life. I cannot wait to see where our futures take us.

Heather, Andrea and Kiki your messages bring me so many smiles, thank you for everything.

Marie N as always one of my biggest supporters, I appreciate you so much.

To my friends Julie and Hayden, as always thank you both for being you.

To my incredible ARC readers and bloggers.

Thank you for all your hard work, messages and support without you I couldn't have achieved what I have so far.

A special thank you to: Nikki, Tasha, Amy, Liana, Lorna and Alluring Lily.

To my mum, thank you for your support. Also, thank you for not disowning me, I'm sure by the next book you will.

To my boys, thank you for everything for being so patient with me.

Dream big boys, I'm proof anything is possible.

To my hubby, the J in my BJ. Thank you for being there.
Without you I wouldn't be BJ Alpha.
Love you trillions.

Thank you to https://www.thesurvivorstrust.org for the information available to myself and others.

I'd also like to thank https://autism.org.uk for the wealth of information available to me and many others.

And last but by no means least thank you so very much to all my readers.

ABOUT THE AUTHOR

BJ Alpha lives in the Uk with her hubby, two teenage sons and three fur babies.

I love to write and read about hot, alpha males and feisty females.

Join me on my social media pages:
    Facebook: BJ Alpha
    My readers group: BJ's Reckless Readers
    Instagram: BJ Alpha Instagram

ALSO BY B J ALPHA

<u>Secrets and Lies Series</u>

CAL Book 1

CON Book 2

FINN Book 3

BREN Book 4

OSCAR BOOK 5

CON'S WEDDING NOVELLA

Born Series

Born Reckless

The Brutal Duet

Hidden In Brutal Devotion

Love In Brutal Devotion